The D at the Gate

The Dog at the Gate

How a Throw-Away Dog Becomes Special

The Dog at the Gate

Published by Pups and Purrs Press
Denver, CO

Library of Congress Control Number: 2017953076

ISBN: 978-0-9966612-4-9

JUVENILE FICTION / Animals / Dogs

Cover design by NZ Graphics
Illustrations by Cathy Lester

QUANTITY PURCHASES: Schools, non-profits, animal rescues, shelters, sanctuaries, and other organizations may qualify for special terms when ordering quantities of this title.

For information, email Sunny@SunnyWeber.com.

This book is dedicated
to the real dogs, cats, and birds of this story~
Especially:
Shadow & Max
Miles
Muffin
Murphy
Mariah
Sheba
Pete & Pepe Parakeets
With love, respect, and appreciation forever.

"Often when you think you're at the
end of something, you're at the
beginning of something else."

—Mr. Fred Rogers

(Mister Rogers' Neighborhood)

Chapter 1

My First Home

"This one! Here's the one I want!" The skinny five-year-old girl squealed and ran so fast, I scuttled back to my mother then hid behind her. I peeked around the snowy fur feathers of Mother's rear legs and watched our people greet the new ones.

"We promised the children a puppy this spring and we've been everywhere. Yours is the first puppy our daughter has taken to," the new lady said. I wrinkled my nose at her smoky smell. She almost dropped the small boy she held in her arms.

"Doggie, doggie!" The lady plopped the boy on our patio and he waddled towards my mother and me with chubby outstretched arms. Barely taller than Mother's back, his dull blond hair stood up in a ragged mass.

"How much do you want?" The strange man towered over us. He stared hard at me then looked at my master. His gravelly voice lacked warmth and his eyes were almost hidden under wiry eyebrows. The man crossed his arms. He glared at our people through one eye and squinted the other eye.

"Max, come." Our mistress waved me to approach.

"Mama?" I whimpered and hid deeper under her belly.

"Obey, Max." Mother's piercing blue eyes stopped me in an instant if I misbehaved but her eyes could also soften with love. I lived for those moments when I knew her attention focused on me. This time she would not look at me. I obeyed and stepped out. I turned my head shyly, blinked my amber-colored eyes, licked my tense lips, and wavered on oversized feet.

"Come, little guy." Our mistress held out her arms. She had always scratched my black fuzzy fur and cooed. Yet I felt a strange uneasiness as I crept forward. I arched my back, ducked my head, and took tiny steps. I turned to look at Mother. Her copper-colored eyebrows slid back over her blue eyes. Her ears drooped. She lowered her head as if she knew something bad was about to happen.

For the past week strange people had come and left with my brothers and sisters. Last night as Mother and I cuddled in bed she said, "I don't know why our people let others take my puppies. At least I still have you." She sighed and gave me a warm bath.

"They'll come home soon." I licked her delicate, milk-white feet and tried to comfort her. I fell asleep cuddled next to my mother's softly breathing belly.

Today strange people were here again. They ignored my mother and only paid attention to me. Unsure of whether or not I should go to the mistress, I raised my brown eyebrows and blinked at Mother. She nodded for me to continue. My mistress picked me up and kissed the worry wrinkles between my ears. I licked her cheek, then glanced over her shoulder. Our master took hold of my mother's collar and guided her into the house. Mother looked back at me as the master pulled her away. The sorrow on her face frightened me.

Our mistress handed me to the daughter. "Here you are, Sweetie. His name is Max. He's a very loving puppy."

The little girl swung me around to face her parents. "I want *this one.* I don't care *how* much he costs!" She stuck out her lower lip, looking like a pigtailed replica of her father. She squeezed me hard against her soiled shirt then put me on the backyard grass.

The girl picked up my favorite red ball and held it high over her head. Distracted from concern about my mother, I jumped on her. The girl threw my ball. It bounced across the yard and the children squealed as I raced off on my big feet to get it. Every time I tried to bite the ball, I missed. When it stopped bouncing, I fell on top of it. I rolled over, got up and claimed it with a paw. I spread my jaws wide and sunk my teeth into the side. Proudly, I carried my ball back. I hoped one of them would throw it again.

The lady laughed and nodded to the man. He looked grumpy. The little girl and boy squealed, "Please, Daddy, can we have him? Please, please, please?" The lady bent down and picked me up. Then these people carried me out of my yard, down the driveway, and away from my mother.

From inside the house, Mother howled, "Goodbye, my son. Always obey your people. I love you. Remember me!"

I barked in my loudest eight-week-old puppy voice, "Mama, come with me!" I am not sure she heard. I never saw my mother again.

Chapter 2

My Second Home

My new family lived in a boxy, egg-shell-colored house with a teeny backyard. I was not allowed in the house but they gave me a bed on the covered patio. Even though the night was warm I felt lonely because I had never been all by myself. At first it was scary, but I was tired from the adventure of coming to a new home and being with new people. I cuddled into the old blanket they had laid over my bed and yawned. Far off I heard another dog bark but it was nobody I knew. My head drooped and my eyes closed. Once I fell asleep I slept soundly until the sun came up.

During the next days my family went away so I was alone until they came home. There was not much grass in my yard and when it rained everything got muddy. No one washed me so

I itched from the dirt that dried out my skin. There were no trees either, so on hot afternoons I squeezed myself into the little line of shade along the dilapidated wooden fence or laid on the hard, cool concrete under the patio roof. I learned how to dig holes and chew on plants to keep busy. I did not have any puppy toys at this house and I missed my red rubber ball.

I barked at people and other dogs that passed the front of our yard. I saw them through holes in the splintered wood. I howled, "Why won't someone play with me? Hey, you there! Come pet me. Hey, dog, how about a wrestle?" I displayed the most inviting play bow I knew but no one could see me behind the fence. I missed my brothers and sisters.

The best part of my day was when the children spent time with me. We ran around and I struggled to keep up. But my uncoordinated, thick-boned legs only resulted in a ploppity amble.

My feet grew too fast, and often I tripped myself as I ran. I rolled over and when I got up to shake the dirt off, my children laughed and ran away again. My efforts to follow them ended up exhausting me. I was too little to play that hard. When I collapsed on the brown grass, my girl said, "Come on, Max, you big baby. You're such a wuss."

My little boy had short legs and could not run as fast as his sister. He seemed to understand and said, "You rest, Max." He came to me wherever I sprawled out and scratched my belly. Pretty soon I had him trained so well that whenever I rolled over onto my back, he automatically scratched me.

"Good doggie. Take nap." I licked his hand and he lay down on the ground with me. We napped together in the late afternoon shadows. My girl just scoffed and left us. My boy and I became best playmates. I suppose we were about the same age. My boy had a high-pitched squeal when he giggled and I tried to do things that would make him laugh. He especially liked a game he called, "Hide and Seek."

"You go hide, Max. I come find you!" He covered his eyes with his chubby hands. Then he counted numbers out loud. "One, two, six, ten, eleben!" His sister told him he did not get the numbers right but neither he nor I cared. When he stopped counting, he dropped his hands and looked around.

Of course, I had no idea what I was supposed to do so I stayed close behind him. I followed quietly as he turned over chairs and peeked behind the trash cans.

What made him laugh that silly squeak was when I poked the seat of his pants with my nose. He jumped in surprise and said, "Oh!

Crazy dog! *You* find *me!*" Sometimes he giggled so hard he could not stop and he fell on top of me in fits. I crashed down on the ground and we rolled around with his arms around my chest fur and me licking his face so he would laugh uncontrollably.

I learned how to read his invitations to play, especially when he giggled that funny way and took off running on his stubby legs. He learned to read my invitation when I did a play bow. I got down on my chest, put my bum high in the air, wiggled, and smiled my widest grin, with my tongue hanging out of my mouth. Then we ran, chasing each other until I bumped my shoulder into his tummy, knocking him down. I always jumped on top of him and licked and licked. He howled, "No fair, Max!" But I just kept kissing him.

Over the months my boy and I played, I grew tall and muscular as my body melded into a sinewy size that fit my legs. My feet became more proportionate and no longer tangled up when I galloped after my children. Soon I could catch both of them. I even got faster than my little girl, although she was taller than my boy and me. I grabbed pant cuffs in my teeth to trip them and then I jumped on top and licked their ears.

"Ick! Stop it, you dumb dog!" My girl wrinkled her nose and put her arms over her head.

My boy giggled and pushed me away. ""Knock off, bad doggie!" He just pretended to be mad.

The master and mistress never played with me. In fact, I hardly ever saw them except through the glass door into the house. They seemed to be no fun for anybody, so my boy and girl and I had all the fun in that family.

When I was alone I paced the boundaries of my yard along the fence. I was bored and curious about what lay outside the wood slats of my tall fence, where I could hear cars roaring and dogs walking by with people. Sometimes a cat teetered on the corner of the front yard fence until I barked at her. Squirrels scampered across the tops of the pickets on their way to other yards and all kinds of birds used the dirt in my yard to take dust baths. They were fun to watch when they rolled around and made little powdery clouds of soot with their flapping wings.

Every day I waited and waited for my children to come home and play with me. My little girl often played with her friends, not me. But my little boy always came outside and spent time with me. He grew longer legs too, and we continued to have fun chasing each other. Sometimes he buried his toys in the dirt and let me dig them out for him. Other times we just sat together on the ground while his fingers stroked my back and scratched my ears. I loved his hands. His gentleness radiated through his tiny caresses.

I was always sad when the mistress called my boy inside for dinner. I liked being with him.

Before he went to bed each night, he brought my bowl filled with my dinner. He talked to me while I ate, then kissed the top of my head.

"Nighty-night, Max, see you tomorrow." I trotted over to the glass door and watched the children go up the stairs to their inside bedroom. Then I curled up on my bed and waited again for my boy to bring my breakfast. I wished I could be inside with him.

Every night I dreamed of my mother and remembered her soft tongue, loving eyes, and warm tummy. Sometimes I woke up in the middle of the night and remembered she was gone forever. Then I cried.

Chapter 3

Snatch

Late one morning after my family had left, a large black bird pecked the ground in my yard after his dirt bath. I wondered what he saw to peck at. He lifted his head from a lump of grass and a fat worm wiggled in his beak. I blinked in amazement when he flipped the worm in the air and then caught it in his mouth. Suddenly he swallowed the worm. I closed my eyes, turned my head away, and thought, "Yuck!"

I heard a burp.

"Howdy, youngster, what's up?" I opened my eyes and looked around my yard to see who had spoken. Would they play with me?

"I say, I say, what's up!"

I jumped to my feet and bounced towards the house. Was someone playing hide-and-seek like my children did?

"Yo! It's rude ta ignore a 'Howdy!'"

I twisted towards the sound of the voice and cocked my head—where could my new playmate be?

The bird was the only creature around. He fluffed up his whole body of shimmering black feathers and shrieked. He tilted his head back and forth and up and down like the paddle ball my children played with.

"Were you talking?" I raised my brown eyebrows. I had never heard a bird talk—they were usually too involved with their friends to pay attention to me.

"Do ya see anybody else in the vicinity, Kid?" The black bird tiptoed, opened his wings and flapped, squatted, then folded his wings neatly alongside his body. His head continued bobbing.

I tilted my head in curiosity. "I'm sorry. You surprised me. Usually nobody wants to talk to me." None of the outside critters had talked to me before. I lifted my ears to hear him better and wiggled my rear end in excitement. Would this bird play with me until my boy got home?

"Whadaya, feeling sorry fer yerself?" His tiny eyes looked like the black stones in our yard.

"No, no, just telling you I didn't expect you to be interested in a dog." I shrugged.

"Listen, Kid. I been watchin' ya fer months. I know yer always alone. Except when those brats come out. Why do ya let them throw rocks at us?" He strutted towards me boldly.

"Gosh, I didn't have any way to stop them." I dropped down to the ground so we could talk eye-to-eye. "I always saw you birds fly away all right so I didn't think about it being dangerous for you."

"I guess I get that," he replied. Then he introduced himself. "I'm called Snatch, 'cause I snatch away and steal shiny things. They come in handy—the girls like 'em. See?" His wings flipped out, flapped and he whipped straight up in the air. He dove behind the fence where our trash cans were kept. He returned in a flash and landed a few inches from my front paws. Then he dropped a small crumpled piece of foil. It rolled toward my front feet as it sparkled in the sunlight.

"My girlfriends love this stuff." He winked one eye.

I smiled at Snatch. "My name's Max."

"Cool. Well, I'm hungry so I'm off to find more delectable bugs and worms. I'll come visit ya, now that we's friends."

"I'd enjoy that. I get lonely when I'm all alone." I smiled, more to myself than at my new friend. I supposed birds can not smile because their beaks are hard. Instead, Snatch winked at me with one eye and then flew away. I shuddered to think he found bugs and worms delectable. I trotted to my bowl on the patio and munched a few pieces of kibble.

Although he was a bird, Snatch would become my best puppyhood friend. His wisdom would guide me in a way my little boy could not. My isolation in the tiny yard would become a sad burden that Snatch's visits lifted. I did not know then that there would come a day when I wished I could fly away with him.

Chapter 4

Yard Dog

When I was six months old the nights turned chilly. My master brought me a flat-topped doghouse and put my bed in it on the patio. After sunset I watched my children play in front of the fireplace through the glass door of the patio. The mistress cooked dinner and even with the windows closed I smelled their warm food. My mouth watered because my food had frozen in my bowl. After they ate, the children played games. I still did not understand why I could not be with them. Why was I left outside?

The days got shorter and cooler winds blew. Dry leaves swirled into the yard and crinkled under my padded feet as I paced my fence line each day. My children played outside less and less and I missed napping in the sun with my boy at my side. He spent more time indoors because he got cold when we were together in the yard.

At night the lights lit me up as I sat looking in, so we could see each other. My boy sat next to the glass patio door inside so he could be near where I sat outside. When it was time for him to go to bed, he blew me a kiss, waved, and went up the stairs. Then the window drapes closed and I could no longer see the fireplace with my family gathered in its warmth.

One evening I smelled unfamiliar moisture in the air and snuggled into my doghouse bed. I had never felt chilled through my thick fur, but the sparkling fog that wafted through my yard made my fur feel damp. Noisy drops of rain started falling and then turned into silent floating white puffs. When I awoke in the morning I was amazed to see the yard carpeted in white, not brown dirt. I tiptoed into the fluffy stuff that came overnight. It was wet and cold and yet disappeared on my tongue when I licked it.

Suddenly my children slammed the back door, ran outside, and my girl hooted, "Snow! Oh boy!" They rolled little balls of the snow in their mittened hands. They threw the balls at each other and me. I pounced after each toss and tried to find mine in the mass that covered the yard.

They rolled three more balls, bigger than the ones they threw. Each was a different size. My girl was strong and she picked up the balls then piled them on top of each other. She put the smallest one on the tippy-top. Then she lifted my boy up and he stuck rocks in the top ball and made a smiley face. My two best chewing sticks were stuck into the middle ball and looked like skinny arms with funny fingers. They giggled and patted the snow hard.

I joined in the fun and peed on the bottom ball.

"OOOO, *dumb* doggie!" My boy covered his mouth to muffle shrill giggles.

"You are *totally* disgusting." My girl wrinkled her nose and stuck out her tongue.

A creak from the house told us the garage door was going up. We heard the car drive in and my children ran to the back door. I galloped after them as they threw the door open. We had been having so much fun and I was so happy to be part of their family, I forgot I was not supposed to go into the house. I raced past my children and leapt into the kitchen. I had lived in my first house with my mother and never understood why I was kept isolated in this backyard. Finally it seemed as though they liked me enough to include me inside their house.

The children's mother came into the kitchen with grocery bags in her arms just as I ran around the corner from the backyard door. My wet paws hit the linoleum floor and flew out from under me. I slid spinning on my side into the mistress' feet. She fell down on top of me. Apples, cans, and loaves of bread flew. Egg whites and yolks oozed out of a box all over the floor. My children laughed and clapped. I got up with a big grin on my face.

But instead of laughing with us, the mistress sat up, rubbed her knee and slapped the floor. On the other side of her I saw my boy's face go from mirth to fear. The pink in his cheeks drained to white. His mouth stretched down with his lower lip stuck out, quivering. His eyes widened and filled with tears. His little body shrunk into a form of dog-like submission. He raised one of his chubby arms over his head as if to stop something falling. Confused, I tilted my head towards him.

Instantly my attention was redirected from him when I heard the mistress yell.

"You stupid dog! You almost killed me!" I gently licked her face. Why was she angry? I ached all over because it hurt when she fell on me but I wanted to show her I was not angry. She wrinkled her face into a scowl. She slapped me away. Then she kicked me farther from her. When she stood up she reached towards my face. Her right hand opened with her fingers spread, like a giant spider. Without thinking but feeling a surge of panic, I ducked my head and she closed her fist on my collar. Her hand twisted my collar so tight I could not breathe. She dragged me to the door and shoved me out. "Stay outside where you belong!" she yelled.

Bewildered, I sat at the door a long time and waited. My ribs ached where the mistress had kicked me but I was willing to be near her if she would let me inside. But neither she nor anyone else let me in. Later my boy brought my dinner and kissed me goodnight.

"Me sorry, Max. Mommy mad." His eyes were red and his nose sounded stuffy. He hugged me a long time and then waddled indoors. He was still humped over and was trying to walk quietly in tiny steps, the way dogs do to appear appeasing and non-threatening. His body posture confused me. Why was he afraid?

After he left I trotted around to the yard and lay in the snow next to the glass door, still hoping someone would notice me. Maybe if they saw me someone would let me in with them. I waited and watched until the family went to bed and turned the lights off and closed the drapes.

I plodded to my doghouse, where I shivered and tried to sleep. I was disappointed and even lonelier that night. What was wrong with my little boy? He seemed unhappy. Was it something I did? Would he forgive me? Why was the mistress mad? Why had she suddenly become so mean to us? Just when I began to feel I belonged to this family, something happened that I did not understand and I was ignored again.

I was never allowed in the house again and the long nights alone were always the worst.

In the dark, shadows of wind-blown branches scared me. As my first winter progressed, the early frigid nights, the muffled quiet of new fallen snow, and my isolation made me wish for the time when I slept in a warm pile of my puppy siblings. I thought about my mother. Where was she? Did she miss me? Was she warm inside our old house with our people? I snuggled into my blankets and tried to pretend they were Mother's soft warm tummy.

The full moon was high over the yard one night when I awoke to clicks and chatters. Toenails on hard dirt, gurgled whispers, and shrub branches cracking brought me out of my troubled dozing. I peered out of my doghouse door and in the glow of the moon saw two large, round, hairy forms skitter across my yard. Instinct told me to be quiet. I watched as the creatures approached the house, the patio—and me.

They sat up with their noses in the air. Their black shadows in the moonlight stretched across the snow and the two looked like four creatures, connected by feet. The largest animal had a black stripe from one ear to the other across his eyes. He dropped down on all four legs and turned in my direction. I backed farther into my house but peeked around the doorway. His beady eyes glowed an eerie green as they flashed from the middle of his furry mask.

The big one trotted around the edge of the patio and sniffed the ground. His nose was shiny black and he had long whiskers that wiggled every time he took a breath.

"Man, I'm starving!" He sat up tall and lifted his nose to the air again. Could he smell me?

"Me too. I smell something dee-liciously stinky!" The smaller creature's nose quivered before he lowered his masked face, wiggled his nose, and followed an invisible trail to the fence around our trash cans. Their claws dug into the splintered wood as they climbed up the wooden barrier. Striped cone-shaped tails flipped behind as they flopped down inside. Lids banged and the cans tipped over with metallic clangs. Paws scratched and ripped through trash bags. Pop cans rattled and paper rustled.

My master screeched open his window and yelled, "Max, shut up! Don't make me come out there." The creatures froze in silence. The window banged shut.

Then the animals laughed and continued to scavenge, creating even more noise. When the back door slammed they quickly climbed back out over the barricade, skittered across the frozen grass, and hid under a small evergreen shrub in my yard.

My master stormed outside in his pajamas. I ran over to show him where the animals had escaped. I jumped on him and bounced away towards the shrub.

I barked at my master,"Intruders! Here they are!"

He did not understand what I was trying to tell him and did not follow. I ran back, took his pajama sleeve in my mouth and pulled.

"Come, I'll show you," I yipped through clenched teeth. I tried to help the master see where the bad creatures went. It was my job to protect the children and our home. He could help me.

"Stop barking, idiot!" My master yanked his arm away and his sleeve tore. I spit out a piece of material and tried again to get him to see what needed to be done. He was bigger than me and could make those bad animals run away. I galloped around and around, bumping him with my shoulder to herd him the right direction. Humans were hard to teach but I kept up my effort to help my master learn. We could team up, two against two, and scare those bad animals away from our yard.

Instead of understanding, the master made a fist, bent down and punched me in the head!

"OOWW!" I squealed, then ran and hid in my house. Why had he hit me?

"That'll teach you. Stay in your house and keep quiet!" My master hissed. His eyes narrowed under pinched eyebrows. Though he seemed upset most of the time, I had never seen him in such a rage. My master pounded back into the house. He did not want to help me save our home and children from the intruders!

Hurt, confused, and afraid, I trembled with a combination of pain, surprise, and disbelief. A dog's job is to protect his home but I did not feel confident that I could handle this situation by myself. But I was by myself. My ears buzzed and my head ached from the master's punch. Worst of all, I heard claws on the concrete scampering towards my doghouse. Those creatures saw me try to tell my master where they were. I cowered and hoped they would not see me. They sniffed in the dark at my doghouse doorway. I remained plastered up against the back wall, cornered and helpless.

"Hey! Coward! Come out here. Scaredy-cat!" The biggest creature's bushy fur sparkled in the moonlight. He was almost as tall as me but was much fatter.

"He's not a scaredy-*cat*, he's a scaredy-*dog!*" said the smaller version.

"And a tattletale! A scaredy-dog with a tattle-tail!" They both laughed in short clipped grunts.

"Please," I begged. "Just go away." I knew I was alone and without an ally. Would they hurt me?

"I'll bite you." The big one sneered.

"I'll take his hind leg if you want the front leg." The smaller one giggled.

I whined. Where was my mother? She would have protected me—now I understood her warnings of so long ago when I wandered away from her. She never liked me to be out of her sight when I was little. I was a silly puppy and had no fear then. This night I knew fear. I quivered uncontrollably as I backed as far into my doghouse as I could. "UOO-UOO-ooo! Help me!" I howled for somebody to save me.

The largest creature looked back to the door that my master had banged out of. "Aww, the dog is too much trouble. That stupid man will come out again. Let's grab some grub and get out of here." They went back to their mess, grabbed something stinky and disappeared over the fence. Would they come back?

Afraid of them—and my master—I stopped howling. Instead I cried quietly and trembled, smashed up against the back wall of my doghouse. I shivered—from the night air, but also from the dark sadness of realizing that I was not loved, or even liked, by the man my mother had told me to obey.

After that I slept only in the light of day. I dozed as birds chirped and squirrels chattered—they would not hurt me. Sometimes I stretched out on the sparse grass in the warm sunshine and fell into an exhausted sleep. I dreamed of my mother's warm nose and cool blue eyes. I dreamed of her kisses and gentle love. I woke up alone and lonely, but out of danger.

Snatch came every day and listened to my worries. "Sorry, Kid. I don't know what to tell ya. I can't help ya at night—birds don't fly then. That's the only time those raccoon creatures come out. Plus, I never liked people—just their shiny treasures."

"YooHoo, Snatch. . ." We both looked up to another black bird sitting on the fence.

"Come on, honey, you promised to take a dirt bath with me." Her voice was flirty and feminine.

Snatch winked at me and flew off.

Chapter 5

Life Lessons

My second spring brought the return of shorter nights and I welcomed the longer days. The sun had just risen one morning when the master brought out my breakfast and put a new collar on me. I had worn my tattered yellow cloth collar for two years and the new plastic collar fit better. It had a small box attached to the collar that touched under my throat.

I licked at the air near the master's face to thank him for my present—he did not like actual kisses. He backed away wordlessly. He so rarely interacted with me that I wanted to savor this moment of his company. I barked to ask him to stay with me a while longer. "*Please* talk to me . . .OOH!"

Pain pierced my throat and stopped my breath. I barked again, "Help!" A jolt of lightning snapped from the box on the collar and shot through me. I tried to claw the collar off—I pawed with my front feet, and kicked with my hind foot but it stayed snug. I could not bark without stabs of painful prickles searing my throat so I whined quietly. I hoped the master would help me, but he only laughed at me.

"Ha, that should keep you quiet. I'm sick of your barking." He turned away and waved me off, showing with his body language that he had no wish to be with me. As he walked away it was plain I was not important.

Still I did not understand. Why would the master hurt me? Is this what all humans did to dogs? Why did humans leave dogs alone in their yards? Why did these people bring me to their house if they did not want me? Why did he yell at me and hit me? Why would he put such a horrible collar on me? Maybe I should not like people. My heart turned cold. I decided to never trust people again.

I knew I could trust my little boy, though. He was too little to be like grown-up people. He was always kind to me and I felt safe with him. We continued to look at each other through the glass door when I was stuck outside and he was stuck inside. My boy always waved at me and smiled—I knew he missed me as much as I missed him. But he could only be with me when the master and mistress let him. We were best friends, like

Snatch and I were, but unlike Snatch, my boy was not free to be with me. The master and mistress bossed him, like they bossed me.

I told Snatch my decision to stop trusting big people when he swooped out of a tree to visit that afternoon. I had been lying forlornly and quietly, waiting for my friend.

"Eh? What did ya say? I can't hear ya." He turned his head almost upside down and peered at me through one eye.

"I'm sorry, Snatch, but you'll have to come close. I can't speak louder than a whisper."

Snatch hopped closer when I pawed the ground in front of me. As I lay low to the ground, I explained my situation.

"Holy Moly! I knowed people was mean to birds but I thought they was nice to dogs." He understood about my feelings for my boy. "Yeah, I get that. He stopped throwing stones at me and sometimes digs up worms and leaves them where I can find them."

I smiled. I had helped dig for Snatch's worms. My boy and I liked to dig together and I was pleased when he left the worms for Snatch.

Snatch fluffed his body and flapped his wings hard. "Hang in there, Kid. Can I do anything fer ya?"

I shook my head. What could a bird do for me except be my friend and listen to my sorrows? Snatch stayed longer that day and when he flew back to his flock, I put my nose under my front paws and missed his sympathy. I even missed his silly foil gifts.

~

The days had become long and hot when a nasty dog moved into the house behind my yard. He wanted to fight me but I did not know why. I asked him his name and introduced myself in my whispery voice, but he only mumbled and gurgled. Large globs of spit hit the wooden boards between us. He threatened me every day. I knew I would never be able to talk loudly enough for the dog to hear me so he could know I was friendly. To avoid him, I never went near that side of my fence. Of course, that made my area even smaller.

Snatch flew into my yard and told me he had watched the new dog from the safety of a tree in a neighbor's yard.

"Listen, Kid. That dog is bad news. His people beat on him to make him mean. They say they want a 'watch dog.' I think he's gone plumb crazy from the hurts. He got sores all over him. Maybe he got no sense. I dunno. Just don't go to the fence and stay away from him."

"Why doesn't he like me? I've tried to be friendly but I don't understand his words."

"Sometimes critters don't like others and there's no way to figure it." Snatch shook his head and flared his shiny tail. "Some cats don't like dogs; some dogs don't like squirrels; some big birds don't like little ones. . .who knows why? I heard people don't like other people if they're different colors or live in different areas." I did not know people came in colors!

"Be careful, Kid. Stay away from that fence. It don't matter why that dog don't like ya. The fact is, he don't. Maybe he don't know why either. Maybe he don't like nobody. His head's not right—could be his people messed his brain up. Maybe he don't hear ya trying to be nice—since ya gotta whisper and all. Maybe he thinks you're ignorin' him."

I felt sorry for the mean dog then, but I took Snatch's advice.

On a late afternoon I napped alone in the sun. Snatch had not come yet so I dozed and waited for him or my boy to come and play with me. When my family was home and especially when my girl and boy were with me in our yard, the mean dog was kept inside his own house and could not try to scare us.

But on this afternoon I heard the dog's toenails click on the hard dirt along his side of the fence and I stayed up near my patio. I drifted in and out of sleep and did not notice when the birds quieted, left their dirt baths in my yard and flitted up to the tree tops. Sleeping lightly, I ignored the routine snuffs and gurgles from the mean dog on the other side. I had learned to be quiet so he would not know when I was near.

Suddenly a splitting screech of tearing wood made my ears ring. I jerked fully awake as the dry squeals of fence pickets splintering shattered the air. I heard the mean dog growl. Then short, throaty barks pierced the neighborhood. I rolled onto my side and looked towards the back fence just as it bent towards my yard. It bounced up and down and I heard the paws of the mean dog hitting it again and again.

When he finally knocked the fence down I saw him for the first time. He was bigger than me with a wide chest, sagging stomach, and narrow hindquarters ending in a bent, pointed tail.

His front legs were shorter than his back legs, which made him look like he was going downhill. His ears looked like the tips had been cut off and he had scars and scabs all over his body. His short fur was dull brown.

When I jumped up to my feet, he did not see me at first. He stopped a moment to look for me through tiny angry brown eyes that were hidden under a thick roll of droopy forehead skin. Then he ran straight at me. As I turned to run away he jumped on my back and tried to bite me on the neck. I rolled over, dislodging his hold. Instead of my skin, his teeth had sunk into my collar and the force of his clench broke through the plastic. The shock collar fell at our feet.

I barked loudly to warn him away but he came after me again. I had no choice but to fight. I flew at him. I got mouthfuls of his mud-colored fur. We wrestled and rolled all over my yard. We shattered the air with the chomps of missed bites. His thick stiff neck kept him from looking up and his short front legs could not change direction quickly. I had the advantage of being more nimble, so I became a tornado of motion. I jumped over him and bit him on the hind leg. Spittle flew out of his flappy mouth folds as he turned.

I let go of his leg, twisted around and smashed him with my shoulder, knocking him off balance. I had a clear shot to bite into the top of his rump. My teeth sunk deep and I finished with a powerful shake of my head. I felt his skin tear in my mouth. The nasty dog shrieked. I smelled blood. Red ooze spilled over his hip.

When I let go and turned for another assault, fear entered his beady eyes and he turned to limp back to his own yard. One of his hind legs dragged. When he moved away something snapped in my brain. I had had enough of everyone being mean to me! Without thinking, I went after him.

I cleared the pile of downed fence in one jump and dropped heavily onto his back. My mouth found his neck right below his skull and I dug my teeth into his flesh. He gasped, then squealed. I shook him again—hard.

Thunk! Something rigid and cold hit my ribs and knocked us both sideways. I slid off the nasty dog and turned. There stood his master, a scrawny man without shoes.

"I'll show you," he spat a human growl. The man stalked forward holding a mud-encrusted shovel. "You tore up my hound. You gotta lesson comin'."

Instinctively, I stood my ground—stiff-legged, chest out, teeth bared, head up, ears forward, silent, and alert. I felt the fur rise on my back from my neck to my rear end.

The man raised the shovel. The rusty metal scoop made tiny circles in the air above his head. His fists turned white on the splintered handle and his flabby underarms quivered with strain. The man crashed the shovel down in a wide arc towards me. I heard a whoosh of air as I ducked. He turned a full circle from the force of his swing—but he missed me. He wavered and tried to regain his balance. He puffed his hollow cheeks with exertion. He staggered, straightened, then raised the shovel in the air again as he stalked towards me.

Defiantly I spread my legs, lowered my head, flattened my ears, bared my teeth, and for the first time in my life, *I growled at a human!*

His eyes widened. He seemed to lose confidence as he waved the shovel back and forth and I sidestepped each blow. I rumbled another primitive, deep-throated threat. For some reason, I was not afraid. He took hold of his dog's collar and backed into his house. His dog limped next to him, gagging from his master's tight hold. The man did not seem to notice or care that he was choking his dog.

I followed, stalking in menacing slow motion. The man with the bully dog slammed the saggy screen door and disappeared. I shivered from sudden fatigue. I had protected myself—and I had won! Revived with this realization, I strutted back to my own yard with my head held high. I was proud of myself as I lay on top of my house licking the blood from my wounds.

"I'm my own dog now and I'm not going to let anybody bully me anymore," I decided out loud. Although I was mad, I was also disappointed—in dogs now, as well as in people.

When my family returned no one came out to see me. Even the children stayed indoors when they got home from school that day. I missed my little boy but I tried to ignore my loneliness. Later my boy came to the patio door and pressed his nose into the glass and waved at me with the little fingers that so often scratched my ears. Tears streaked his rosy cheeks. A hand appeared from behind the drapery, grabbed my boy's arm and pulled him out of my sight. The drapery closed.

I knew my boy was powerless. I knew he wanted to be with me and I missed him. I felt downhearted at our situation, but I was beyond crying. I had cried enough.

When everything had quieted down, Snatch landed on the corner of the flat roof of my house next to me.

"Mymymymy! Ya poor Kid!" His shiny black head shook and shook. "You done good to protect yerself. I saw the whole thing and I'm a witness to yer self-defense."

"I appreciate your support, Snatch. I will never be able to make grown-up people happy or to like me, so I've decided to give up. I'm my own dog now and I'm not going to let anybody boss me anymore. I want to be free like you. I wish I could fly away with you."

"Be careful what ya wish for, Kid. Every situation has its good and bad sides. You have food plopped in front of ya when you're hungry and a house in the rain. Birds gotta hunt all the time and we live outside, no matter what the weather."

"Yeah, but you have bird friends." I fought tears when I thought how lonely I felt for a dog friend. I missed my mother and brothers and sisters. I missed playing with dogs who understood our own language and knew dog games. My children played with their own human friends more and more and not with me. Snatch was a good friend but I did not understand his attraction to girl birds and foil.

"That's true. Hang in there, Kid. I seen nice dogs in yards. That one ya beat up ain't a good example." Snatch hung his head and looked at me through his left eye.

I only sighed. I wanted to believe Snatch but I did not have the energy to hope he was right.

Chapter 6

Rejected

Late afternoon shadows were long in my yard on the day of my dogfight and still no one in my family had come out to me. A strange car arrived and parked in front of our house. Red bumps on the top of the car lit up and flashed. Through a gap in the wood fence I saw the man who got out of the car was dressed in black and wore a hat with a shiny silver thing in the front. Another silver thing shone on his chest. He went in the front door of our house and stayed a while. I went back to my perch on my doghouse. When the man left my master stormed out into my backyard, shook his fist, and yelled at me.

"I told you to behave. Now you've done it. You're stupid and spiteful. You're a vicious, worthless mongrel!" I remained on top of my house, put my nose in the air, looked away, and ignored him.

I had no idea what had made the master so angry again. I had given up trying to figure him out. I did not understand any of his words—they were just long strings of angry sounds to me. I fought my loneliness for my boy and continued to harden my heart towards my master and all big people.

That evening my stomach ached but no one brought my dinner. Even my little boy did not come to kiss me goodnight. I refused to whine at the glass door and the draperies remained closed so I could not see inside. I decided if no one brought my breakfast in the morning I would dig under the fence and find something to eat by myself. Somehow I would escape and see the world. I wanted to find my mother. I knew she loved me and I knew she would understand that I had tried to follow her command to obey my people. But I just could not do it anymore.

The sun set behind the mean dog's house when I jumped off my dog house roof. I rolled in the dirt of my yard, then stood up and shook the dust out of my fur. My ability to trust flew off my back and out of my heart like that dust. I was all grown up at two years old. I felt strong, proud, and wise. Trust and love had no place in my life. My only concern was survival. Food, safety, and freedom became my new goals. Self-confidence welled up in my chest and I spent the moonless night on top of my doghouse, not cowered inside.

I planned my escape for the next day when my family was gone.

My master came out in the morning. I boldly looked into his face, but did not leave my perch on top of my doghouse. I had slept there all night for the first time. I was no longer a frightened puppy and I did not ask for attention or affection.

The master was unaware of the change in my attitude and he did not bring my breakfast. Instead, he put on my tight old yellow collar. I refused to look at him. Then he surprised me. He tied a rope to my collar and dragged me out to the front yard and to the car. I had only been in the front yard and in a car once, when they took me from my mother and brought me here. I balked. What was he up to?

"Get yourself in this car, you stupid dog. I've had enough of you." The master grabbed my fur, picked me up and threw me in. I stifled a cry when my head hit the top of the door and spasms shot down my spine. He shoved me farther in, across the back seat. My left ear scraped along a tear in the seat and my head hit the opposite window. He slammed the driver's door after he got in, and jerked the keys. The motor sounded like an angry growl as we screeched backwards out of the driveway.

In the big front window of our house my little boy appeared. His cheeks were shiny and wet again. His eyes were red and he pounded on the glass with the palms of his hands. I jumped up on the back of the seat to see out the rear car window. My boy kept pounding with one hand and waving frantically with the other. His mouth moved as though he was screaming, but I could not hear him. I held a whine inside my throat. It distressed me to see my little boy upset but there was nothing I could do. I was imprisoned in the car speeding away from him—but to where?

I continued to stand on the seat looking out the rear window—down the street I had not seen since the day I arrived. Three houses away Snatch drank from the gutter with his girlfriends.

Some of his friends hopped in the sprinkler water that drained over the sidewalk and flowed past my house. The sparkling trickle in the gutter was my lifeline to my friend. But he had no way to know I was in the car.

I wanted to talk to Snatch and to listen to his advice. He had a special way of calming me and I would have preferred his company to my angry master's. I watched Snatch flap his wings and strut around the girls until he became a speck of black far away. We turned a corner and I lost sight of him.

The master careened down another street. When we squealed around a sharp corner, I felt dizzy and fell down onto the seat. My stomach convulsed and I threw up what little was left in my stomach. The car stank.

"For Pete's sake, you dumb dog! You've ruined the car!"

Then the master made the windows go down. Suddenly, fascinating scents entered my nose. I smelled flowers, fresh soil, and dogs in yards we passed. I saw trees, streets, and houses slide by. The wind fluffed my fur. I had never been brushed, so the feel of fresh air on my skin tickled. My ears flapped in the cool wind and I heard birds squawking and singing.

We stopped for a moment and I saw a cat stalk a mouse in the grass, as a squirrel watched from an overhead tree branch. After being confined in my backyard for two years, I had no idea the world held such treasures for my nose, eyes, and ears. I forgot my nausea and hunger.

The car lurched forward again. We drove by children on bicycles. Their laughter reminded me of my children. I remembered how fun my children were when I was a puppy. I thought about the sad and panicked look on my little boy's face as we left. It reminded me of the sad look on my mother's face as she was led away from me the last day I saw her.

We finally parked in front of a wide white building. I heard dogs barking and howling. Frightened, yet lonely for my own kind, I wondered if my brothers and sisters were here. I could trust them. Would Mother be here too? My heart leaped with hope for the first time in a long time.

"Get out!" The master opened the door, jerked the rope and choked me. I jumped down. "Come on, mutt. I can't wait to be rid of you!" I could not remember a time when my master was not mad at me. I ignored him and looked around as a strange uneasiness gripped my chest. My hope disappeared.

I did not like this place—even from the outside, it was noisy and smelled like dog pee. I felt a surge of anxiety as my stomach knotted. Not only was the smell repulsive, the volume of unhappy dog voices made me feel there was something sinister about whatever lay beyond the front building where two glass doors led into. . . what?

I leaned back on my haunches, which tightened the pull on the collar around my neck. My master dragged me through the doors and into an office while I gagged and struggled to go back to the car. A roly-poly lady in thick glasses came out from behind a desk and took the rope from my master.

"Come, Max," her childish voice cooed. "I won't hurt you. Here, take this." She offered me a food treat. My stomach growled so I left my master's side. Greedily I swallowed the food and turned back to my master. He had disappeared.

Chapter 7

Shelter Dog

The roly-poly lady put me in a long enclosure outside the building. "There you go, Max. We'll take good care of you here and you'll make friends." She took off my tight old collar and the rope and gave me a new paper collar with numbers on it. Then she clanked the latch of the metal gate behind me.

I was loose but to do what? And to go where? The chain-link fence towered over me. The floor was concrete. Enclosures like mine imprisoned other dogs up and down a long aisle. Bowls of water and food waited for me near the gate. My empty stomach churned but I hesitated—was this a trick?

At the end of my fenced area, right across from where I stood quivering and drooling, a dog-sized opening was cut into another building.

A growl drew my attention and a small dog appeared in the doorway. "Not again," I thought. I hated to fight but I would not let this pipsqueak deter me from the food. Keeping the other dog in sight, I gulped down each mouthful.

The little dog let me finish eating, then she approached slowly. She held her head down and did not look directly at me. Her stubby tail wiggled in a shy manner. This polite welcome made me hold still and lower my head, but I remained on guard. The little dog had short white hair with black spots. She had big bulging black eyes and the shortest nose I had ever seen. It was smushed up with wrinkles, and looked like someone had punched her nose into her face.

"My name is Puddin'. I'm a Boston terrier. I lived here with a Beagle named Suzy. Suzy left last night with a new family. You're big and frightened me. Are you mean or nice? You don't have a tail to tell me what you're feeling."

Dogs communicate with tail motion but I did not have one. Australian Shepherds like me have tails but people cut them off right after we are born. They think we are too new to feel pain, but we do. It hurts. People think we look better with "docked" tails, but it is easy for other dogs to misread our intentions.

I told Puddin' about the nasty dog I had fought. "I can take care of myself, but I'd rather not fight."

Puddin' was friendly and sweet. It was nice to have a dog friend at last. I could let down my guard with this innocent and kind girl. As Puddin' and I got to know each other, I relaxed in her company. It was good to be able to speak my own language and have someone understand.

We played and lay in the sun. We talked about how confusing humans were. Puddin's mistress had left her there too. We waited for our people to come take us home. While we waited, we shared our life stories. I fought back tears when I told her about my little boy. But I stiffened when I explained what the master was like.

"My master yelled at me," I said. "I tried to understand what he wanted, but he never made sense. He put a collar on me that hurt when I barked. He hit me with his fist. He didn't feed me when he got mad." I shook my head.

"How awful for you," Puddin' replied. "My mistress hit me too, with a rolled up newspaper. It made noise and stung my skin. She scared me because she was much bigger than me." Puddin's usual cheerful face changed into a frown. She wrinkled her forehead, sniffled, and continued her story.

"We lived in a little apartment so I didn't have a yard. My mistress took me out mornings before she left and evenings when she got home. I learned that she wanted me to poop and pee when she took me out, but the sidewalks were hard and I got splashed with pee whenever I squatted. I hated that. My mistress never explained what she wanted, she just yanked my collar. My neck was always sore.

"When she went away, she left me food, toys and water. I played, slept, ate, and looked out the windows. But I was still lonely. I had a favorite place on the carpet where I peed. I didn't get splashed then. I pooped behind a potted plant in the living room. The carpet felt as good as grass to me."

"Why did your mistress bring you here?" I wondered why someone would leave a charming dog like Puddin' in a place like this. The people here were kind but every dog wants a special person to love. And a real home of their own.

"My last night with my mistress, she yelled at me. She'd been gone a long time. She hollered and took me to the potted plant. She stuck my nose right into my poop! Some of it got in my eyes. I cried and then hid under the couch so she couldn't reach me." Her bulging black eyes flooded and bubbly tears slid between her lashes and her wrinkled nose.

"Why on earth would she do such a thing?" I felt sorry for Puddin'. She just shook her head and shrugged.

"When my mistress brought me here she cried and kissed me before she left. Do you think she'll come back?"

"Humans are unpredictable. Their moods confuse me." I tilted my head in sympathy.

"Human moods *frighten* me!" Puddin' shivered.

"It must be doubly scary for you. At least I have a chance to defend myself. Some humans are afraid of dogs my size." I remembered how the man with the bully dog retreated into the house when I growled at him. Puddin' was small-boned and fragile. She would be easy to hurt.

Puddin' sighed. "I don't know the answer. I don't want to be scared. I just want to be loved."

"Me too." Admitting I wanted love again made me feel melancholy. I knew I would never again know the love my mother and first family had shared with me. Puddin' and I laid our heads on our front paws and heaved simultaneous sighs.

Every day we dozed outside in the sun on the rough concrete. The pebbles on the ground dug into my elbows and hind legs. I slept better on grass or a pillow. Even the bare dirt in my last yard was more comfortable. Puddin' tried to stay outside with me as long as she could bear the concrete. When it made her little bones ache, she went inside to our straw bed. It was too hot in there for me.

Although we preferred absorbent surfaces like grass or soil, we had to pee on the pavement in our run. Once again, Puddin' faced what she hated. After she peed, she would hop away from her wet spot and get as far away as she could, shaking her paws in the air. We had soft straw in our shelter house but we did not want to pee on the straw we slept in. Mother dogs teach their puppies to go potty far away from their bed and our mothers had raised us both with manners.

At night the dogs in the shelter barked and made it hard to sleep. Every one of them had stories of unpredictable behavior by humans. Some were "lost and found" dogs. Some were brought there by their owners and abandoned like Puddin' and I had been. Life in the shelter made me uneasy and I longed for the familiarity of my old threadbare yard. At least I knew what to expect there. Puddin' and I, and all the dogs, waited for our families to come take us home.

One afternoon a bent old lady came and made a big fuss over Puddin' through our fence. One of the shelter ladies opened our gate and picked Puddin' up.

"Puddin', this is Mrs. Snow. She'd like to get to know you." She handed Puddin' to the old lady. The lady held Puddin' in her arms and talked to her in sweet tones. She kissed Puddin' on the cheek and stroked her back.

"What a cute little thing you are. My darling Dewie died and I can't live without a dog. We'll be happy. Would you like to try? Come home with me. We'll have a good life."

She carried Puddin' away. Puddin' barked, "Goodbye, Max! I'm not afraid. I hope you find someone nice to take you."

Although I was happy for Puddin', I was broken-hearted to lose her friendship. Would anyone ever hold me with affection?

Chapter 8

Butch

I lived alone for a couple of days. Then a ragged black dog was put in with me. He sat at the gate of our run shivering. I introduced myself but he turned his head away and would not budge. He did not talk or tell me his name. He refused to eat. I offered him a bowl of food but he did not go near it. That night it rained. I went into our shelter and slept in the straw. He never came in. He continued to sit by the gate and got drenched. By morning he was so weak he could not get up and the people took him away.

They put a skinny Doberman in with me next. He attacked me immediately and I fought back. The noise of our battle brought shelter workers running. He was taken away too.

Later that afternoon they put an Airedale in the run next to me. The Labrador Retrievers that had been there, a brother and sister, had left that morning with a new family. After the new fellow was settled in, I came over to his side of my fence and introduced myself once more.

"Name's Butch," he replied. His raspy voice made him sound like a tough guy.

"I saw the shelter people bring you. Did you just arrive?" I had never seen a dog like Butch.

"Na, I been down da row in a bigger run but they needed da space fer a newcomer and her ten puppies. Her people dumped da whole kit an' kaboodle shortly after da pups were birthed. Poor thing. She's missin' her human family."

Butch tilted his head and scratched at his small floppy ear with an angular hind leg. Then he straightened and shook. His skin was loose and rotated around his torso. His clipped hair looked wavy and wiry. He was copper-colored and had a black saddle-shaped spot on his back. One side of his face and the ear he had scratched were also black. He had a white patch on his chest between his front legs and his docked tail stuck up like a six-inch stick.

"Did your family leave you here too?" I cocked my head.

"Na, I been runnin' loose before people caught me an' brought me here. I lived with a cruel man. He used to beat me. He used his fist, sticks, anythin' dat was handy an' hard. So I ran away." He cleared his throat with a gruff hack.

I pricked my ears. "You did what I planned to do! Were you scared? How did you do it? Did you find it difficult to be alone?"

"I was kinda scared. New things can be unnervin'. But I was fed up with bein' mistreated, so it was da best thing fer me to do. I dug a hole under da fence. I couldn't jump high enough to go over. It took me a week to make da hole big enough. I dug behind a lilac bush so my master wouldn't see. When I finished diggin,' I turned sideways an' pulled myself under an' out."

Butch dropped to the ground, clawed at the air, and wiggled to show me how he had slid under his fence. I felt the excitement of his escape.

"I wandered a couple of days then met a lost dog named Tiger. We traveled together." Butch shook his coat again. "We was crossin' a street one mornin'. We didn't know it could be dangerous. We both been inside cars but never around movin' cars." Butch's forehead wrinkled, his ears dropped, and he stared at the ground.

"Tiger was an old cocker spaniel with short legs. He couldn't move fast enough. One of da cars hit him. He dragged hisself to da side of da road. I tried to help." Butch whined. His stick-tail drooped and he lowered his head.

"I licked him an' nudged him." Butch's nose moved back and forth as he mimicked how he had tried to help his friend.

"Tiger stayed dere with his eyes closed, whinin' quietly, an' then he stopped breathin'. I hid in da shrubs an' watched people come look at Tiger." Butch sniffed and pawed at his wide nose with a bear-like front paw.

"Da people saw me an' called to me. They offered me food. I was hungry so I went to dem. Da people took me to a vet. Da doc fed me regular, den brought me to da shelter. He said I'd find a family." Butch tilted his head. He knew he might never be chosen.

Most people liked fluffy puppies and smaller dogs like Puddin'. The Labs that had just left were young and outgoing and bouncy. Butch was old, his fur was rough, and he was large boned and ragged. His long, skinny legs and big feet made him look clumsy. His head was boxy, not cute and rounded. His square face gave him an air of aggressiveness. His personality was straightforward and gruff.

"When I came here, I heard da humans refer to certain dogs as 'killed.' People kill mean dogs. Dat grumpy Dobie's a goner." Fear crossed his face. Then his tough, independent look returned. He shook himself once again.

What made the Doberman so mean? Would I become that mean? I had hardened my heart but I would not attack anyone without a good reason.

"I been here a long time." Butch's forehead wrinkled. "Dere are too many homeless dogs an' not enough humans who'll adopt us." Abruptly he walked away and disappeared into the building and his straw bed.

Homeless? Is that what I truly was? Suddenly I understood. The pride I had felt when I won the dogfight crumbled. People had all the power. My family had abandoned me forever. It became clear they were never coming back for me. I realized I would never see my little boy again and my eyes filled with tears. One or two dripped down my nose before I jolted myself back into control. After all, I had decided I was not going to let people hurt me anymore. But my resolve did not work. I was in a prison of chain link fencing and emotional disappointment. I collapsed on the concrete next to my gate and sobbed quietly.

After our first day together, Butch and I talked a lot. He was a strong, wise, and compassionate old man. We discussed our past lives and how we viewed the humans we had known.

"I was born in a junkyard an' was expected to guard da area I was fenced into with my mother. I had a brother an' a sister but both of 'em were taken away."

Just like mine had been!

"Da mean man I belonged to beat my mother to death one day—right in front of me! She was very old then an' had no strength to defend herself. I don't know why da man was mad at her.

He hit her with an iron pipe. I think he was just tryin' to scare her but instead he hit her head an' she collapsed before I could run to her. The man seemed a bit sorry to have lost one guard dog, but did not seem sorry to leave me there alone." Butch's eyes were angry but filled with tears.

"It was shortly after my mother's death that I decided to escape. I knew da same thing coulda happened to me."

Both of our mothers had been the only true love Butch and I had known. At least I had my little boy and Snatch as friends. Butch had Tiger for a little while. Butch was kind to all the other dogs in the shelter and as each one left with a new family, he was sincerely happy for them. He always remained optimistic and hopeful for the rest of us too.

I respected Butch. He patiently listened kindly to everyone's stories, and gave wise advice. He never felt sorry for himself or dwelled on his own tough past. Despite his size, age, and appearance, we each hoped that some kind person would take Butch. But it did not happen.

One rainy day a volunteer took me for a walk. When I returned to my place Butch was gone. "Butch! Butch, where are you?" I ran back and forth along our shared fence. Was he in his straw bed? Was he out for a walk somewhere that I did not see him? An awful, uneasy dread filled my heart. My instinct told me something bad had happened to my friend.

Tip, a long-haired mixed breed dog on the other side of Butch's run told me gently, "Butch's time was up. No one wanted to adopt him so they took him away to be killed."

People took Butch away and I never got to say goodbye!

I paced Butch's side of my run sniffing the fence, the ground, and the air. Each day I repeated my ritual until the people's cleaning eliminated every morsel of Butch's scent. I curled up next to the fence and gently pawed the mound of grass that grew through a crack in the concrete. Butch and I used to take turns eating that grass, just like we shared our thoughts, fears, and experiences. I mourned the loss of a dog who deserved love but never found it. No one would know that such a special creature had existed. Butch was gone forever and would not even live on in someone's heart or memory, except mine. I knew I would never forget him.

I lived at the shelter a long time too. I paced and wore my toenails down on the concrete until they bled. I howled at night. I could not sleep. I had no power over my destiny. People did what they wanted with dogs. People could be nice or mean. They might feed us or starve us. They were able to love us or kill us. Butch was brave, compassionate and smart. Yet no one wanted him. So they killed him. Would anyone ever want me?

Chapter 9

"Time's Up"

The weeks passed and I was terrified that the people would kill me. They were nice to me, but they had been nice to Butch too. Until they took him away and killed him. I did not trust any of them.

There was no way to escape so I went back to mindlessly pacing the confines of my fenced run, like I had paced the fence line of my old yard. I paced and paced. I could not sleep and even thoughts of my mother no longer comforted me. I lost my appetite. The bones poked out of my skin and my fur lost its luster.

I did not want to become friends with other dogs. If they were adopted I would never see them again. I could not face losing another friend to death either. Dogs came and went. Some were mean, others depressed, others friendly and confused. Only I remained the constant occupant of that run.

Mindlessly I trotted, morning, afternoon, and night. I became weaker and less coordinated. I fell in my poop and pee while I paced. I smelled disgusting but I did not care. My footpads bled as I wore the skin off but I was oblivious to the pain. There was nowhere to go but up and down the fence.

"Hey, Buddy! How are you today?" On a hot spring morning a volunteer hosed my bloody footprints off the concrete. She was a gangly, red-haired, freckled girl, who always took time to talk. I stood aside, hung my head and panted from the heat and anxiety. I did not understand her words and refused to trust her. Her lilting voice was a distraction from my loneliness, but still I closed my mind to her sing-song friendliness.

"Goodness, look at your footprints. Let me clean your feet." I leaned into her to balance as she picked up each paw and ran a trickle of cool water over my shredded footpads. I relaxed a bit in her gentle touch.

"I think I'll bathe you too." She pulled a bottle of liquid out of her supply cart. "Boy, are you filthy." She did not seem to notice my remote attitude and rubbed my fur until it became a mass of bubbles. A fresh scent surprised me and then I realized—it was me! I had never had a bath.

As the red-haired girl rinsed the shampoo and hummed, the shelter supervisor walked up to the gate, raised her hand, curled her finger and wagged it. The girl turned off the hose and wiped her forehead with the back of her hand.

"I hope you don't mind, but I took the time to shampoo Max. Look how shiny he is! I'll clean the run now."

"Don't bother," the supervisor said. "This one's time is up. They come for him this afternoon. You can clean after he's gone."

My stomach churned. My head ached. My mouth went dry. I could not breathe. I heard ringing in my ears. Anguish exploded out of my mouth in a high-pitched howl. I threw myself at the gate. "No, no! Look at me. I want to live!"

The girl put her arms around me and asked, "May I call Australian Shepherd Rescue and see if they can take him? Max has so much life in him—he's young and healthy. I hate to see another wonderful dog wasted."

The supervisor shook her head. "I wish there were enough rescue groups to save all of them!" She glanced down the aisle at the other runs with hopeful faces and wagging tails behind the chain link fences. "There are just so many. . ." The supervisor frowned and wiped her eyes with a rag from her back pocket.

The girl nodded, frowned, and rubbed her hands on her shirt. "Please let me try to save Max," she pleaded.

"Go make your call. I hope they can help." The supervisor waved towards the main building and turned away.

"I'll call Aussie Rescue right now!" The red-haired girl took my bloody front paws off the gate and patted me on the head. "I'll be right back, Buddy." She flew into the office. I was embarrassed that I had showed them how afraid I was. But I also knew I wanted to live. I wanted to find someone to love who would love me back. My pride crumbled in the realization that my life could be hanging on what the red-haired girl did in the next few minutes. I trembled uncontrollably.

When she returned, the girl picked up the hose and said, "I'm going to finish cleaning, Buddy. I've left a message and I hope the rescue has room for you." She smiled and stroked my back. I was not sure what she meant but the return of her happy words comforted me a bit.

No one came to kill me but I could not eat my dinner. What would tomorrow bring? That night my heart bumped against my chest. I could not catch my breath. I paced. When I did lie down my legs jumped uncontrollably. I ran back and forth along the fence. The dogs on either side of me complained that I kept them awake and they retreated into their straw beds inside.

I was left to face my panic, confusion, and desperation by myself. I had not allowed myself to make friends since Butch's death and no one tried to comfort me. And so I paced. I tore my feet open again and left a fresh trail of blood along each fence boundary. I fell again and again in my exhaustion but I could not stay still. Stinky filth clung to me, overpowering the fresh smell of my bath just a few hours ago.

Despite my new stench, the night was filled with the fragrant scents of early season buds. I stopped every now and then, trembling, and looked up at the white moon that spotlighted me. Stars twinkled, and a soft breeze fluffed my fur, yet I howled my sorrow. Where was my mother? Could she see the same moon? I longed to be a puppy snuggled next to her in our old yard under the buds of our lilac shrubs. She would never let anyone harm me. She would save me if she were here.

The next day was bright and hot again when my red-haired girl led a pretty blond lady to me. I jumped up on the gate. My bloody feet left fresh red paw prints on the chain link.

"Save me!" I yipped. Even if I never found love, I did not want to die. The girl opened the gate and the blond lady put a leather leash on me. What was going on? Was this new lady taking me to be killed? I froze in place.

"I'm glad you called," she told the girl. "The poor thing is a bag of bones. Look at his feet. I'm glad we have a foster home available. When puppy season starts, foster homes for the bigger dogs get harder to find."

The red-haired girl stroked my bony shoulder. "Goodbye, and good luck, Buddy." She smiled warmly at me.

I licked her hand to show my appreciation for her kindness then pivoted out the open gate towards the exit door of the shelter, and bounded forward. I dragged the blond lady in my panic to escape. If she tried to kill me I planned to pull hard and run away. Instead, she held tight to the leash.

"Settle down, Big Guy. You pull too hard. Everything is going to be all right now. No one will hurt you and we'll have you settled soon." Although I did not understand her words, her tone of voice did not sound like the other people who took dogs from our runs to be killed. Usually they were ominously quiet, or impersonal and detached. Her voice was soft and kind.

Once outside the shelter, I saw the paved parking lot and beyond, trees, grass, and *freedom*. There was no one waiting to kill me. I ran around and jumped on the blond lady to show my gratitude.

"Thank you for saving me! Thank you, thank you!" I drooled and panted.

"Come, Max. It's time to start a new life." She took me to a van where a tall brown-haired lady opened a cage door.

Oh, I had not thought this far ahead! I suddenly felt unsure, then frightened. I did not want to go in another vehicle. Would this trap take me to wherever they took dogs to die? I froze again and would not walk forward.

The tall lady greeted me. "Hello, Max. My, what a big Aussie you are. Hop in and we'll take you home." *Home?* What home?

I whined and looked back at the shelter. I remembered my anxiety when I first came. Could a new place be any worse? I took a deep breath and decided to take a chance. I jumped into the cage and the ladies latched the grate then slid the van door closed. Inside I smelled the scents of many dogs. Was this a good sign? I quivered, panted, and drooled, then threw up but nobody yelled. Where were they taking me? I could not see out. What was this "home" they spoke of? I wanted a permanent, forever *real* home.

Chapter 10

Rescued

We finally stopped. The ladies opened the van door. I smelled green grass, and through the wire cage door I saw a two-story white house with large trees. Tall vines and evergreen shrubs surrounded the front porch and flower boxes were under the windows. I heard birds and saw a squirrel stop and stare at me before it scooted up a tree trunk.

The yard smelled like freshly cut grass and moist soil. The flowers' scents floated to me on a happy breeze and their overlapping sweetness calmed me a bit. The blond lady put the leash on me again. I jumped to the ground and tried to see and smell everything at once.

"Let's go for a walk and stretch your legs." The blond lady smiled and stroked my head.

We wandered up the tree-shaded street and passed other dogs behind fences who barked at me.

"Hey, where ya goin'?" asked a tan and white terrier mix.

"You're new around here, aren't you?" A Dalmatian stood with his front paws on top of the chain link fence encircling his yard.

"Can we come? Tell your person to come get us." Two Chihuahuas chimed in unison. They peeked through the wooden slats of their white picket fence. I did not answer—I was so excited to be free, I did not know what to concentrate on.

The tall lady met us when we were several houses down the street from the van. She brought two dogs with her—one a black, brown, and white colored Aussie like me, the other a ground-hugging black thing.

The other Aussie said, "Hello, my name is Miles. Will you stay with us?"

"I don't know what the ladies are going to do with me." I raised my brown eyebrows.

"Well, if you do stay, I'm the boss!" boasted the little dog. She stuck her nose in the air and raised her scraggly tail high. It looked like a question mark wobbling in the air, but there was no question of her dominant personality.

"My name is Max." I looked back at Miles. I tried to return his smile but my lips quivered with nervousness.

"This is Muffin. She's a poodle-mix." Miles tilted his head her direction. Muffin snorted and trotted away. Her round rear end swayed on top of her skinny bird-like legs and teensy feet.

Miles and I scratched the ground and took turns peeing on shrubs. Muffin balanced on her front legs, with her hind legs in the air, and shot pee as high as she could on the bushes. I laughed at her. She glared at me. Miles's body language was relaxed, friendly, and welcoming. Muffin's was haughty, stiff, and stuck-up.

After our walk the ladies turned us loose in a wide fenced backyard behind the white house. There were bushes, trees, lush grass, tasty bones, and wonderful smells. Best of all, there were balls! Big ones, little ones, soft ones, hard ones, and ones with bells! It had been two years since I had a ball to play with. I ran around and mouthed each one. I felt like a puppy again! Running free at last, I forgot to act like the sophisticated grown-up dog I wanted to be.

Overhead, birds were all around me. I looked into the trees while the birds' various songs and calls echoed throughout the yard. There were bird feeders and baths by the wood fence but when I ran to them, the birds flew away. I sniffed the air.

"What are you doing?" Miles trotted up behind me.

"I'm looking for Snatch, my best friend. He's a black bird. Do you know him?"

"I'm sorry, I don't. He's never been here." I had no idea how far we had travelled so I knew the odds were that I would never see Snatch again.

"We'll keep an eye out for your friend," Miles said.

"It's been so long since I smelled green grass, trees, and fresh air! I'd forgotten how sweet a yard could smell." I closed my eyes and took a deep breath. This place reminded me of my first home where I was born.

"There is a field just outside our wood fence where we go every day. There are many wonderful smells there too," Miles said. He sniffed me politely and wrinkled his nose but did not say anything.

Muffin joined us, walking purposefully with her nose up, like a big shot. She sniffed me too and said, "You stink!"

The ladies called us back to them. "You'll be safe here, Max. I'll see you again sometime," the blond lady gave me a chewy treat. She scratched under my chin, smiled, and then went out the gate. I heard her van drive away.

We spent my first day at the new house outside. The tall lady sat in a chair and read a book. Later she put water in the birdbaths with a hose. She let me copy Miles and catch some water on my tongue. She played with flowers, and did what she called, "chores." After a day of relaxing in the yard, she fed us dinner—in the house! I was beside myself with joy—it had been over two years since I had been allowed inside a house. I felt overwhelmed and unsure of how to behave. I jumped on the furniture, twisted in circles and bounced from room to room. I wiggled my tailless rear end and even kissed Muffin on her cheek in my mindless exuberance.

"YEEUCK!" She spat, then bent her head down to the rug and rubbed her face while she pushed forward with her rear end in the air. Her body was in a play bow but it was clear she was not inviting me to play. Instead, she scooted along, mumbling noises of disgust.

"That was pretty funny, Max." The new mistress covered her mouth with her hand to hide her smile from Muffin, but her crinkled eyes showed me she was not mad.

"Haven't you ever been in a house? Settle down and we'll relax together. Here is a chew bone. Lay down here on the rug in front of the fire." The night had cooled and a small blaze cast a bouncing light on Miles' back as he accepted his bone. Muffin savored hers among the toys in the corner basket. The mistress' voice was amused and kind as she laid my chew in front of my feet.

At last! I was inside a house with a real family, in front of a fireplace!

Miles smiled at me. "The mistress thinks you're funny. She likes you," he told me. My heart leapt with hope. I decided to be quiet and polite. I wanted everyone to like me so I could stay inside and not sleep outside in the yard all alone. I chewed bones with Miles and Muffin while my new mistress watched television stretched out on the couch.

Three other creatures also lived in the house. I saw their small faces behind the baby gate in a doorway. Miles saw me watching them.

"They are cats," he said. "The big stripy one is Mariah. She sticks to herself. She tolerates us but isn't outgoing. The black and white one is Murphy. She and I grew up together. She's dignified but bossy. She'll pop you on the head if she doesn't like what you're doing. Straighten up then, because if you don't, the next pop will be with her claws. The little gray one is Sheba. She's blind and skittish but nice."

"I've never been close to cats. I chased them when they were on my fence at the old house." I felt my legs quiver with excitement but I forced myself to lie still.

"We're not allowed to chase them. They're our friends so we treat them with respect." Miles grinned.

"So don't get any big ideas!" piped in Muffin. "If you even raise an eyebrow to frighten them I'll tell the mistress." She was still mad at me for laughing at her when she peed on the bush.

I just watched the cats. After a while, Murphy jumped over the baby gate and crept toward me. She kept her body stretched out and her ears pointed my direction. She remained ready to bolt if I made an aggressive move. I forced myself to lay still and put my head on my paws. That way, my eyes were the same level as hers, because she was little. She inched closer.

My eyes were the only parts of my body that moved. Finally she touched my nose with hers. Little puffs of air came from her tiny pink nostrils and her long, fine, white whiskers tickled my coarse black ones.

"Hello, Dog." Murphy whispered, still ready to run.

"Hi, nice to meet you."

Murphy backed away, turned and jumped onto the mistress's lap. The mistress smiled at me. She had been watching us. "Very good, Max," she nodded. I sensed her approval.

"It's okay, girls. He's nice. You can come in now." Murphy swished her tail. I repeated my greeting with Mariah when she boldly walked to me. After we touched noses, she said, "Hey."

"Hey." I did not know cat manners so I copied her greeting. Mariah jumped on the back of the couch. Her tail flapped against the wall and made a thunk, thunk, thunk sound.

Shy blind Sheba stayed away. She paced back and forth behind the baby gate. Sheba obviously wanted to join her family but she was afraid of me. I rolled onto my side and half opened my eyes so I could see through my eyelashes but still look asleep—I forgot Sheba was blind.

After I had been still for a while I saw Sheba gracefully and silently jump over the gate. She slinked under the end table then tiptoed behind me. I felt the gentle nudge of her curious nose on the back of my head between my ears. Then Sheba retraced her route, jumped up on the couch and crouched low between the mistress' outstretched legs. It amazed me how Sheba could figure out the room and me without being able to see.

At bedtime the new mistress turned on a small light in the family room and put me in a big plastic dog crate to sleep. It was smaller than my old dog house and I felt cramped. I was unable to stretch out my legs and I did not like the roof over my head. It was impossible to see out the back at all. I felt cornered. What if somebody came to hurt me in the middle of the night? Could raccoons get into a house? Did cats get mean in the dark?

Miles, Muffin and the cats went upstairs with the mistress to sleep. Why couldn't I go where they did? I sat in the dark and listened. I could not remember the last time I experienced such quiet. There were no dog barks or howls, car noises or yelling people. An overwhelming exhaustion crept up my spine, weakened my legs and threatened to slow my thoughts. I fought the peacefulness of this house and was determined to stay alert. I did not want to let my guard down. If I fell asleep, I would be vulnerable. I tried to stay awake, to listen, and watch. My mind churned with anxiety and foreboding. Would I be allowed to stay here with Miles, Muffin, Murphy, Mariah, and Sheba? Would tomorrow be the day they killed me? Would I be taken to another prison?

In the semi-dark silence my eyes drooped and my front legs gave out. I dropped down on the soft pillows in the crate. My worries tapered off and I fell into a deep sleep. I dreamed of my mother, brothers, and sisters in our old bed.

Chapter 11

My New Life

I awakened to chirps from two tiny parakeets who lived in a big cage near my crate. I had never seen birds in a cage before. They were covered up at night but as soon as the morning light came through our window shades, they began little chirps, as though they were whispering to each other. I heard the floor creaking upstairs. Then I heard the mistress' voice and Miles' and Muffin's claws on the wood floor as they came downstairs.

"Good morning, Max." The mistress chirped almost like the birds as she opened my crate. "I hope you had a good night's sleep. Thank you for being so quiet." She seemed happy to see me! Although I could not understand her words yet, I could tell she was not mad at me for anything. "Come on, Big Guy." I popped out of the crate, stretched all my legs, arched my back, and shook my fur. Miles and I exchanged sniffs.

"How did you do?" he asked.

"This house is so quiet I fell asleep and had the most wonderful dreams! I haven't slept in a house since I was eight weeks old. Good morning, Miss Muffin," I looked at that fuzzy little black face and lowered my head to be polite. Perhaps we could get off to a better start today.

"Hummmpf!" Muffin stuck her head in the air and trotted towards the big glass patio door. Her tail was stuck up, just like her attitude.

We went outside and the mistress stood on the edge of the concrete and spoke to us. I had no idea what she wanted.

"Go potty." Miles ran to the ash tree and peed. Muffin circled a shrub then squatted on the grass in front of it. I stood next to the mistress and watched them.

"Max, go potty," she repeated. I looked up at her, cocked my head, and wrinkled my forehead. What did she want me to do? The mistress repeated her command in a kind tone.

I was about to burst open so I ran through the grass to Miles' ash tree and lifted my back leg. I had never been locked up all night and unable to pee whenever I wanted to. I peed for a very long time! Then I ran back to the mistress on the patio and looked up into her eyes. I hoped she would not be angry that I left her. Instead of being upset, she praised me.

"Good boy, Max." The mistress smiled and clapped her hands. Somehow I had made her happy. We went back into the house for breakfast. I hesitated at the door, remembering how upset the last mistress was when I followed the children inside.

"Come, Max. Inside." This mistress held the door open for me! I lowered my head and politely stepped past her.

The mistress prepared three bowls of dog food for us and set them in separate corners of the kitchen. I had not eaten inside a house since my siblings and I had scrambled for kibble while my mother looked on. This second meal inside a home brought my appetite back. I happily ate mine and looked up to see what else this wonderful morning would bring.

After feeding us dogs, cats, and parakeets, the mistress moved around the kitchen preparing her own food. Miles finished eating and laid down. Muffin left some food in her bowl and went to beg for bacon from the mistress at the stove. When Muffin's back was turned I sneaked over to eat her leftover food. Muffin saw me approach her bowl, bolted and bit me on the nose.

"Get your ugly mug out of my food!" She bared her teeth, squinted her eyes, and flattened her ears. I did not know if I should attack her or ignore her.

The mistress turned. "Max, this is your bowl." She tapped my empty bowl with her cooking stick. "It's only yours and it will always be in your corner. You must leave the other dogs' bowls alone. Are you still hungry? Here's some more food."

She scooped more kibble out of the container, smiled and stroked my head.

"You can have as much as you want. You're way too skinny for an Aussie." I wolfed down the additional breakfast and licked the mistress' hand. Would she hit me for licking her? I looked down again to be polite.

The mistress surprised me by kneeling on the kitchen floor, taking my face in her gentle hands and kissing my nose. I kissed her back. She smiled at me. She scratched my ears and blinked her eyes without staring at me. I had never known a human who understood dog language. She was trying to be polite *to me!*

"Thank you, Max. Now be a good boy and go outside and play with Miles." I watched Miles pivot and dash through a small plastic covered hole in the bottom of the laundry room door. I followed him but stopped in front of the hole. I could not see through the plastic cover. I cocked my head back and forth. How had Miles disappeared?

"Come on, Max. Push the cover with your nose. I'm right outside." I followed Miles' instruction. Slowly I stuck my nose, then my face, then my ears out the door. The cover easily gave way so I could see where Miles was. What a surprise to find myself in the backyard! I never knew a door existed just for dogs. I never again had to be locked alone in a yard. If I wanted to go in, I could. If I wanted out, I was free to go.

Miles and I trotted around the yard, peeing on trees and shrubs. I chose a ball and carried it around, chomping and tossing my head. When I dropped it, there was another one, waiting for me.

What joy it was to feel soft soil and lush grass beneath my shredded footpads, instead of hard concrete. I flopped down and rolled and rolled. Miles laughed and then joined me. It was warm where the sunlight shone, and cool where the tree leaves shaded. I had missed the beauty of nature, even though I had only known it once—in my first yard, while I was still under my mother's watchful blue eyes.

Muffin had stayed inside with the new mistress. Muffin still did not like me. Her grumpy attitude reminded me of the nasty dog at my old house and the aggressive Doberman at the shelter. But she was so small I was not sure how to deal with her. I expected tiny dogs to be afraid and easy to intimidate, but she was not. And she sure was not as sweet and friendly as my good friend Puddin' had been.

After Muffin bit my nose that morning, the mistress shook one finger at her and said,

"Muffin, you're getting too big for your britches." I did not know exactly what that meant but it seemed Muffin had done something the mistress did not approve of. I decided to be patient with Muffin. If I tried to fit in and make everyone like me, maybe they would let me stay.

Later that day the mistress told me, "You smell terrible, Max. Let's get you cleaned up." She scrubbed me in a big bowl she called a bathtub, and brushed my fur. I loved feeling clean and being touched with affection. I had only experienced that one hose shower at the shelter and I was amazed how light both cleanings made me feel. It was almost like the loving baths my mother used to give me.

The mistress used special conditioner that took away the itch in my skin and made my fur shimmer. She put medicine on my toenails, massaged my feet, and put a new red nylon collar on me with a brass heart-shaped tag.

"This tag has your name and our address and phone number on it," she explained. "If you get lost, people will know where you belong."

Belong? Did I finally belong somewhere? I bounced outside through the dog door to show Miles and Muffin. Miles already had a teal collar and Muffin had a pink one. We all had brass identification tags. I felt snazzy.

"Look at me!" Muffin and Miles were sniffing the base of a locust tree when I trotted out. They looked up. I pranced around, lifting my feet high with each step and stuck my nose in the air.

"Very nice," smiled Miles.

"Oh, big deal." Muffin said as she turned her rear end to me.

I told Miles about the shock collar at my old house. He shook his head.

"Our mistress would never use such a thing. When she teaches us to do things, she rewards us. Fear is not a good way to get a dog to do something. We obey because we *want* to, not because we *have* to." I did not understand his explanation but was happy I would not have to wear another one of those awful collars again.

No one came to kill me. Instead, my first week in my new home was full of lessons. The mistress taught me the basic laws of her world. Our daily routines became familiar. Kind, firm, and attentive, like my mother had been, I felt happy to know what she expected and to be able to earn praise. There was much I did not understand but instead of yelling at me, my mistress helped me see what she wanted with hot dog treats, praise, and patience.

I told Miles, "I have not tasted a hot dog in three years. When I was a tiny puppy at my first home my master taught me how to sit by holding little pieces of hot dogs over my head until my bum fell onto the ground. Then he praised me and popped the hot dog piece into my mouth. I learned to sit a lot. Whenever I was around him I practically scooted on my rear end. He laughed and always had hot dogs in his pockets."

Miles laughed. "We have all learned tricks with hot dog rewards. Sometimes we get cheeses too."

I did not know what cheese was but at last this one glorious delicacy was back in my life, and in my mouth, again! I would do anything for hot dogs!

Miles and I got along great. Outside we chased each other and wrestled. We were both Aussies and therefore herding dogs, so we tried to push each other with our shoulders. We play-bit each other's legs, bumped each other with our hips, jumped up on our hind feet, and tried to knock each other over with our front paws.

Muffin and I competed for attention and toys. I knew she was the boss and I let her bite me when she felt like it. It did not hurt anyway. Sometimes I took her toys just to make her mad. In a fury, she jumped up and bit the ruff around my neck but her teeny mouth could not get past my thick fur. I walked around while she hung from my throat. She growled in anger and I just laughed. Miles watched and giggled.

The mistress taught me about leashes. I had to sit patiently for mine to be put on. The leash meant a walk in the park or the field behind our house. At first, I did not understand how to sit still. If I failed to sit quietly the mistress put the leashes away and no one got to go. Then Muffin got mad because we lost our walk. The mistress returned in a few minutes and we tried again. I learned to control myself to earn the privilege of a walk.

At first, I pulled and jumped and ran. I jerked the mistress so she got me a head halter. When I pulled at the end of the leash, my head turned around and I ended up facing backwards. I could not walk backwards and I wanted to face forward and see where I was going. Everything was so new and interesting. The head halter was not painful and it did teach me not to pull. Miles and Muffin were smart. They walked with no leashes sometimes and followed all the commands the mistress gave. I wanted to be that smart.

Once out of our yard gate, we had a large field to run and play in. Muffin and Miles got to run off-leash because they knew all the mistress' commands and obeyed. I was still learning so I had a long leash that allowed me to run in a big circle around my mistress.

Sometimes we walked up and down the hills in the field and sometimes we crossed the field and went to the grassy park that was attached to it. The park was full of big trees with manicured lawns and flowers. The field was wild with tall grasses and small shrubs. Birds lived in both places and so did rabbits.

The field was bigger than the park and was home to funny little critters that lived in the ground called prairie dogs. Sometimes we saw deer and occasionally we saw a dog-like animal far away, looking at us.

Miles told me, "That's a coyote. They are a type of wild dog and are quite unpredictable. We must stay away from them and respect their natural ways. If they have puppies they can be protective and dangerous. They eat rabbits and prairie dogs, but sometimes they will eat cats and small pet dogs too." We both looked at Muffin. She had been listening intently but when we turned to her, she put her nose in the air and refused to show fear.

"They're not so scary," she huffed, and turned away.

"Our mistress has taught us to appreciate wildlife and we are never allowed to chase anybody, not even a goose, duck, or rabbit," Miles continued. I was fascinated because I had never been in such a big, wide-open place or seen wild animals in their natural habitat. The mistress allowed me to sniff prairie dog holes but I was not allowed to dig down them.

"Those little dogs aren't really dogs. They are what are called rodents. They live underground, Max," she explained when I tugged at my leash. "There is a whole town with tunnels connecting rooms down there. Some rooms store their food, some are where their babies are, and some are gathering places for the whole family. We must respect their homes as we would want them to respect ours.

"Prairie dogs are very smart and have a complicated language. They can tell each other when a predator is coming and if it is a flying danger, such as a hawk, or a ground danger, such as a domestic dog or wild coyote."

I tilted my head and pricked my ears at my first prairie dog hole, trying to hear what was happening down below. My mistress laughed and then said, "Come on, Max. Let's walk on."

People came to our home and played with me. Miles said, "Our mistress is a professional dog trainer. Our house is a 'foster home' for homeless dogs like you. People come and look at the dogs that stay here with us. If she likes the people, she lets them adopt the dogs."

Was I still a homeless dog?

"But I want to stay right here! The mistress gave me a collar and tag. I thought that meant I had a home at last," I wailed to Miles.

"She puts collars and tags on all the foster dogs. Don't worry, Max. She'll find you a good home and won't allow anything bad happen to you." Miles nudged my ear with his nose.

Could I be given away again? Would the mistress kill me if nobody wanted me? What would become of me? I wanted a permanent home with a forever family. Most of all, I wanted to stay with *this* family!

Chapter 12

Special Dog

The months passed. Other Australian Shepherds came to stay with us and then left with new families. I remained the one no one wanted. I could not believe this mistress would kill me. I refused to think about it. Instead, I concentrated on learning the new skills she taught me. She taught me many human words and the dog action that she wanted with each command, such as, "sit," "come," "walk with me," and my favorite, "Good dog, Max!" I wanted to be praised and loved. I tried to do well.

The mistress and I practiced car rides and I did not throw up anymore. I learned to love rides because the car took us someplace fun and I had the mistress to myself for a while. One day we drove to a place I had never been. We went into a big room with pictures of dogs on the walls, rubber mats over the floor, lots of equipment, and toys. It smelled of disinfectant yet I could tell many dogs had been there.

A small man met us. He spoke to me gruffly but with a twinkle in his eye. He had sparse blond hair forced into a flattop style, wore jeans, hiking boots, and walked with a prideful strut, with his toes turned out. I could tell he loved dogs. He knew right where to scratch me and he had delicious treats in all his pockets. I liked him right away.

The mistress and I practiced the new things she had taught me. The man watched. She asked him, “What do you think? Max is a *working* dog, not a *pet* dog, right?”

The gruff man looked up at my tall mistress, smiled slyly, and shook his finger at her nose. He said, “If I were you, I’d adopt that dog. That dog needs a job and he’s a perfect competition dog. He’s high energy, intelligent, and pushy. Exactly the opposite of what people want in a pet dog. If you train him from scratch with my methods he’ll win every time. He’s a special dog!”

A special dog. No one had ever said that about me!

A couple of days later the blond lady from the van came to our house. She and my mistress wrote on papers and the mistress gave the blond lady money. Then with big smiles they called me to them.

"Look, Max." The mistress showed me the papers. "These are official adoption documents. You're part of our family. You have a permanent home!" Relief washed over me because she seemed so happy. Did this mean I was safe? Did this mean I would not be killed? Could this family love me?

We celebrated with hot dogs, hugs and kisses. The mistress never minded my kisses and even sat on the floor so I could reach her. She taught me the word for kisses. Whenever she wanted one she asked, and I delivered!

Our mistress showed no favoritism between us. When Muffin and I had a tiff, she let us work it out. If we lost our tempers, the mistress separated us in different rooms for "time outs" until we were patient with each other again. She never sided with one or the other and treated us equally.

I could tell Miles was her favorite though—they shared a special bond. They had been together for many years. He was a "pet" dog type—easy to be around, quiet, gentle, and a bit shy. I could see he adored our mistress and it was clear he had never been mistreated, lonely, bullied, or frightened. She had made sure his life was the best any dog could hope for, from the moment they met when he was a small puppy.

Muffin's over-confidence probably made her take the mistress' affection for granted. Only I had known hardship, rejection, and ridicule. I knew better than to take anything this family gave me for granted.

The mistress treated me wonderfully and Miles remained humble and good company. Muffin continued to boss me. Sometimes I submitted to her demands and other times I ignored her. I was so thankful to be included in a family at last, I accepted my pack position.

I joined Miles and Muffin with our mistress at the gruff man's school. I watched my new brother and sister in their classes, and then I had my turn. I tried hard and found hot dogs, cheese, and praise were my rewards. My mistress was deliberate in her movements and rarely confused me with her verbal commands and body language. Most people say one thing but their body language says something different. Dogs communicate with each other by body signals and my mistress knew this. At last, I understood what to do and what not to do.

I never imagined my life could be so wonderful.

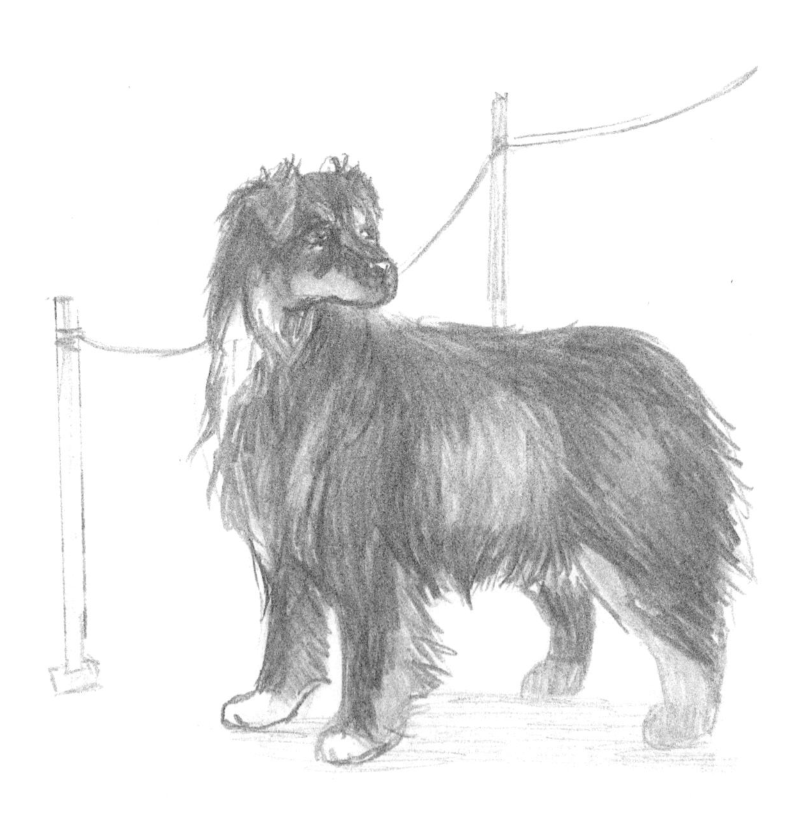

Chapter 13

Dog Shows

One morning the mistress woke us up early. The parakeets were still quiet. We ate breakfast then jumped into the car.

"Where are we going?" I asked Miles.

"To a dog show." Miles settled into his corner of the backseat.

"What's that?" I climbed into my corner and yawned.

"We compete in obedience contests. All the things we've learned at school will be tested. Other people and dogs perform and we try to beat them. You'll see. You and our mistress are a team. You must obey her and ignore everything and everybody outside the show ring."

"What's a show ring?" These new terms piled up in my head.

"You are so brainless!" Muffin shook her head. I saw her frown through the grate of her crate in the front seat.

I ignored her and turned back to Miles. He smiled and explained, "When we do our tricks there's a judge who watches. The show ring is an area we're in and is bordered by a square of poles holding a rope fence. You must stay inside the rope and do what the mistress tells you. Activity outside can distract you and cause you to miss a command. Don't look or listen to anything but the mistress."

Another new challenge! It was hard for me to concentrate because after my two-year confinement in a tiny yard, I wanted to take in all I could absorb in this new life. I hoped I could focus only on my mistress and not be distracted.

We drove a long time. The day had warmed under a cloudless sky as we arrived at a large, flat, grassy park. Hundreds of dogs and people milled around. The mistress set up our crates and equipment under a shady cottonwood tree. She told us to wait in our crates and she walked to some tables. I did not mind the crate anymore. My mistress always returned to let me out and nothing bad ever happened to me while I was in it. We watched as she talked with the people at the tables and received papers with big black numbers. One was for Miles, one for Muffin, and one for me.

We each had a turn when our mistress took us into the show rings. I was last. I did my tricks for the judge. I paid close attention to my mistress' requests. I remembered Miles' advice and focused on my mistress' eyes.

After all the contests, the judge gave out ribbons. Miles won a blue, Muffin received a red, and I got a green. The mistress said, "I'm proud of you, Max. Even though you didn't win, you got a qualifying score your first time out. That's unusual. You *are* a special dog!" I was happy because she was happy. We went home and returned to our regular life.

The judge in my second show was a dark-haired man in a western suit. He wore a tall white hat with a wide brim that shaded his eyes. I found it difficult to not stare because I had never seen such a thing on anyone's head. I could not stop looking. I tried to pay attention to my mistress but I kept sneaking peeks at the funny-looking man and the big hat.

Suddenly I felt a rope around my neck! I gagged and jumped back, forgetting the man and his hat. Disorientated, I turned to look for my mistress but she had disappeared from my side.

Behind me, she stood facing the opposite direction but her body was half turned, and she was looking back at me. Disappointment radiated from her downturned lips and puzzled eyes. My mistress had turned on the judge's command and trusted me to stay at her side. Instead, I stared at the man's hat and forgot to pay attention. I missed her signal to turn and ran into the rope. We were disqualified because I touched it. My mistress snapped on my leash and we left the ring. People shook their heads and said, "Too bad. It takes time for a dog to learn to concentrate long enough."

The mistress never said an unkind word. She said nothing at all. I was crushed. She put me in my crate and left. I did not sense that she was angry but I was disappointed in myself. I was ashamed that I had let my wonderful mistress down. I hung my head and fought the tears burning in my eyes.

"What happened?" Miles was in his crate next to mine. I told Miles what I did. He shook his head in sympathy. "It's true. It is hard to concentrate. You'll learn and do better next time. Cheer up."

"Boy, you are one stupid dope!" Muffin sneered from her crate on the other side of me. "Who ever heard of being distracted by a dumb hat?"

Anger began to rise in my brain, instead of shame. "You were never distracted by a hat because you're too short to see that high," I retorted.

"All right, you guys, hush up." Miles nodded towards our returning mistress.

We went to dog shows every summer weekend. I won more ribbons. Occasionally I lost my concentration and did something wrong. I either won or ended up disqualified. My mistress and the gruff school man continued to work with me. When I messed up, they repeated my drills over and over until I finally understood. When I performed correctly, they praised me. I felt stupid and frustrated when I made mistakes. Was I a slower learner than the average dog? Would I ever be as smart as Miles? I was still afraid the mistress would give me away if I could not learn to pay attention.

I practiced at home. In the yard I stared at a bone or a ball, focusing as long as I could. Often Muffin ran out of nowhere and picked my object up in her mouth, spun in circles, and threw it far away. Her interference made me mad so I chased her but never caught her. She hid under things I was too big to crawl under.

"Na-na-na-na-na-na," Muffin teased. I lay down next to her hiding place and practiced staring at her. That made her mad and enabled me to get back at her. It was easier to practice staring when I knew she was trapped. Getting revenge on her was great motivation for me.

We attended more classes and I learned more complicated tricks. I enjoyed the challenge of figuring out what my mistress and the gruff school man wanted. I relaxed, focused on my duties, and my concentration improved. I became accustomed to the commotion at shows and was not afraid of other dogs.

Still, I worried. I wondered if my value to my family was due to winning ribbons. What would happen if I continued to have concentration problems? Would Miles finally make fun of me? How could I earn Muffin's respect if I failed? Would my mistress trade me in for a better competitor? Would she kill me?

Nights before a dog show I was shaken awake by bad dreams. Nights after a dog show I slept soundly if I did well, but had more nightmares if I had goofed up.

Chapter 14

The Big Time

Ten months after my adoption the mistress left Miles and Muffin home and took just me to a huge dog show. The concrete coliseum had giant round pillars that held the roof up. Windows high on the sides of the walls allowed sunlight in to flood the floor. The show area smelled dank but intrigued me with overlaying scents of dogs, people, and vendors who sold dog products. My mouth watered every time we walked past booths with food.

"The largest area is for 'Showmanship.'" My mistress pointed to a congestion of dogs, people, and show rings. "These dogs are the best physical examples of their breed. They stand in line and trot in front of a judge. Then they're given ribbons for just being pretty. What you do is more difficult and takes far more work. You have to be smart." My mistress respected the accomplishments of working dogs.

But what an assortment of breeds! There were itsy-bitsy critters I found hard to believe were dogs; there were giant moving hairballs with legs; there were colors of every combination and pattern from stripes to spots to blotches. Dog voices varied from high-pitched, ear-splitting yaps to deep, booming woofs that shook the air and echoed off the walls. Some dogs had no voices. Their owners had debarked them with surgery. They sounded raspy but did not let the lack of volume deter their efforts to voice their opinions about everything.

Upstairs there were other show rings for "Obedience." This was the area I recognized. Each ring held equipment I had learned to use to do my tricks. We set up my crate and then my mistress brushed my fur. She had bathed me the day before and my black, white, and copper fur shimmered in the overhead lights.

A loud voice announced my contest. Suddenly I smelled an unusual odor. It emanated from my mistress. She was nervous! I had never known this in her—she was usually easy going and calm. Dogs can smell even the slightest change in emotion in their people. Sensing my mistress' excitement I became alert, and anxious too. Would this show be my undoing? If I failed would my fate be another shelter? Would someone kill me if I goofed up? My stomach knotted. I panted with anxiety. My sides heaved. My legs quivered. My eyes watered, ready to overflow with tears of worry.

As we stood waiting to enter the roped area, I glanced up at my mistress. She looked down, smiled, winked, and said, "This is the Big Time, Max! Let's show them how it's done."

I smiled back. I could do it. I might not be the smartest dog in the world, but with our routines in my head, I knew what she expected. I blinked, took a deep breath, gulped, and trotted forward with her next to me. My legs steadied, my stomach calmed, and my head rose.

With only a judge in the ring with us, my mistress and I performed our tricks. We synchronized without words. My past life became a blurred memory. The commotion outside the ring disappeared into a mindless murmur. All I saw were my mistress' body movements and her eyes, which spoke to me fluently, kindly, and encouragingly. I flowed through each task as though the knowledge had always been buried within my bones. When we left the ring my mistress kissed me.

"Nice job, Max. I'm proud of you." She led me back to our waiting area and we both sat down and waited for the other dogs to compete. I felt I had done well, and as long as my mistress was happy, I was too.

We returned to the show ring when it was time for awards. Inside there were already three Border Collies. I was the only Australian Shepherd. Carbon copies of each other, the Border Collies had powder white neck ruffs and feet, fluffy long black body coats, and faces with white blazes. Border Collies are extremely intelligent and know it. They stood at their handlers' sides, heads high with smug panting smiles, bushy tails waving.

My mistress and I took our place at the end of the line and all of us faced the judge in the center of the ring. The judge's back was turned to us and he was talking with people who were behind some long tables just outside the ring. Everyone seemed to be waiting for something.

"Hey," said the Border Collie next to me. "Look at this." He nodded his head to me but looked at the others. "What kind of mutt is he? He doesn't even have a tail." He waved his flag-like tail to make fun of me.

The Border Collie at the end of the line said in a lilting feminine and insulting tone of voice, "Maybe a pound dog?"

The one in the middle looked me up and down with contempt on his face and replied, "Probably a filthy stray." He snapped the white tip of his tail.

I had been rejected and homeless like they said, but I was not anymore. Still, their ridicule shook me and my confidence crumbled. I felt shabby and out of place next to the shiny, silky-haired Border Collies. None of them had ever lived without baths, and been ignored, unloved, starved, or rejected. The smugness of those who lived pampered, easy lives oozed out of their perfect fur, finely shaped but mean faces, and fancy collars and leashes. I was sure they had never been bloodied in dog fights, shocked senseless with inhumane collars, threatened by wild creatures, or ever been hit by a human.

I looked up at my mistress. She looked down at me. She winked. I wiggled my tailless rear end in response. "Let those Border Collies say what they will, I am what I am," I thought.

With my mistress at my side, I was prepared to face any bad names those snobby dogs might call me. She had told me how beautiful I looked as she prepared me for this show. If I was beautiful to her, that was all that mattered to me.

I knew how lucky I was. My mother had taught me love so I could recognize it when I saw it again. Although there had been a long time of misery before I found love once more, I had been given a second chance at life while other dogs, like my good friend Butch, were not. I owed it to Butch and all the others who never found good fortune and love to do my best. I wanted to show those snobby Border Collies and everyone that shelter dogs can be as good as anybody!

I ignored the Border Collies and put my complete trust in my mistress—the one who had saved my life. Through my mistress' faith in me, I had found my purpose in life. I was meant to be her companion, her loyal follower, her devoted friend. I would do my best to never let her down.

The judge was finally handed a piece of paper. Silently he looked at it and the human voices in the room quieted. Suddenly the judge shouted into the microphone, "We have a winner!" I jumped when I heard my name and my mistress' name echo around us. Wild cheers and claps came from the crowd.

My mistress whooped and jumped up in the air. I had never seen her act like this before and did not know how to respond. She bent over and gave me the biggest hug. We were supposed to wait until we were out of the ring to touch each other. But she grabbed me and praised me in front of the judge and everybody! I felt like the luckiest dog in the world.

When the commotion died down I heard the story of my life told to the crowd.

"Max was abandoned in a shelter by his first family. They said he was unruly and disobedient. He was a *throw-away dog* and one day from being euthanized. Max was saved by Australian Shepherd Rescue. Max's owner fostered him and spotted his desire to learn.

"Just ten months after being adopted, Max is our new 'High-In-Trial' winner. He has outscored every dog he competed against. He is the best dog in the country!"

Renewed cheers and claps made me jump again. My mistress stood beaming with happiness and patted me hard on the shoulder.

"I love you, Max! You are such a *special* boy." She clapped her hands to show me I had done well. It was a hand signal that she saved for only my biggest accomplishments.

I had never known ecstasy like I felt at that moment. After all the years of sadness, loneliness, and cruel treatment, everyone seemed to finally like me. Now even a stranger said I was the best dog. I had found my special person, my own family, and I realized that at last, I had accomplished all my goals! My life was full of everything any dog could want. My dreams as a puppy came true as an adult dog. Such success was hard to absorb in my mind and my heart. At that moment, I wished I had a tail because if I did, I would wag it until it broke! Instead, I wiggled my rear end so hard and fast, I stood on my tippy-toes.

My mistress walked forward and I followed at her side. I held my head high and even tried to raise the stump of tail I had left. The judge handed my mistress a gigantic ribbon with colored streamers. She received a certificate with a fancy golden seal and a big silver cup filled with dog treats.

We trotted around the ring to deafening applause and I smiled my widest grin. When we went past the Border Collies, they dropped their tails and heads. They would not look at me now. I had won this competition and proved I was smart. The approval of the crowd showed they respected my accomplishments. Once again I felt safe. I had re-earned my place in the family.

I trotted out of the ring at my mistress' side with my head high. My mistress' pleasure was the only reward I really needed. This perfect day ended with cheers for me and my best friend, savior, and life partner, my own beloved person.

Chapter 15

Team Work

In the summer the plants in our yard, field, and park were abundant with various sized leaves. They provided cool places for us to lay in and each leaf had its own scent. Brilliant colored flowers overflowed their beds and spilled into emerald grass. They too, had many smells but I had to be careful when I sniffed them—sometimes there were bees collecting their lunch!

The bees bounced from blossom to blossom eating, and itsy-bitsy flying bugs gathered in clouds drifting on the slightest breeze. All kinds of birds flew in and out of nests in the overhead branches, and baby birds called to their parents. Some days the asphalt walking trail in the park was too hot for our footpads so the mistress guided us to the cool grass on our walks.

The grass held a variety of scents also and we trotted from tree to shrub, sniffing to see which of our neighborhood dog friends had been by. One particularly perfect day Miles suddenly stopped trotting, raised his head, and sniffed the air. I copied him. There were so many scents. I did not know which one concerned him.

"Uh-oh," he said.

"What's wrong?" I asked.

"The Chow dog is around and I don't think he's in his yard."

The Chow was nasty. He tried to attack us when we passed his house on the park trail. His backyard had a high fence but he could see us through the wire. He lunged, growled, and said mean things. Our mistress kept us close whenever we went by. We had already passed his yard and all had been quiet. Now I knew why.

Miles was right. Over the crest of a hill, the Chow approached with rigid, aggressive body posture. His head was up, his nose in the air, his ears pricked, and his tail curled over his back. His gait was a stiff-legged prance. He was alone, no human accompanied him, and he was roaming freely. Miles and I stopped walking. We faced the Chow's direction, our noses twitching.

Our mistress saw us freeze. "What is it, boys?" Her gaze followed ours. "Close! Come closer, my puppies." Muffin looked up and she too saw the Chow swaggering towards us. She scooted over. Although we were on our long leashes, our mistress never pulled and choked us. She told us what direction to go in, to stop moving, or to come to her. When we had gathered beneath her gaze, she told me to sit on her left, Miles to sit on her right, and Muffin to sit between her feet. Once together, we all concentrated on the Chow.

Miles told me, "We'll be a more sizeable group like this. Sitting is a neutral body posture between dogs. We don't want to challenge the Chow. Don't growl or move."

"Hmmmph! I don't think he's so tough!" Muffin sat tall with her little chest stuck out.

When he saw my family, the Chow ran straight at us. We held still. Before, when a dog attacked me, I protected myself. Now I had to obey both the mistress and Miles to keep us all from harm.

"Get him!" barked foolish Muffin.

"Muffin! Quiet!" The mistress spoke sternly. Muffin dropped her head. She was embarrassed but also scared now. The alarm in the mistress' voice frightened her.

"I'm sorry," she whined softly. Muffin hated it when the mistress disapproved of something she did. Our mistress had never sounded so stern. I knew from her voice and the aggressive approach of the Chow that we were in danger. We were in real trouble. We sat and waited.

"Everybody stay," whispered our mistress. She stood up straight and spread her arms a bit to make herself look larger.

The Chow arrived and puffed out his chest when he stopped in front of us. "What have we here?" The Chow growled as he began to circle us. His black-skinned lips curled into a sneer that outlined his sharp white teeth.

Our mistress spread her feet, and lifted her arms away from her body to make herself look even bigger. Miles and I sat up straighter. The fur on our shoulders rose and we sat as tall as we could. We tried to appear more intimidating. But we said nothing. Muffin leaned into the mistress' right leg.

"What's the matter with you *wimps*? Are you dominated by your person? No one controls me. My people do what I want or I have a say in it." He gave a throaty, gurgling growl.

"Let's have it out!" He hissed through bared teeth and squinted eyes. He taunted us as he trotted around making low gurgling noises. He reminded me of the mean dog on the other side of the fence when I was a puppy at my old house. My skin crawled from my memory of my first dogfight. My heart thumped with an initial burst of fear, but I regained control of my thoughts. I had won then, and I would win now. Then, like now, I would not initiate a fight, but if one was started, I would protect myself and my family.

I choked back the initial nervousness, lifted my head high, and waited.

We watched the Chow's every movement out the corners of our eyes but we did not make direct eye contact. We knew he was looking for any excuse to fight. Direct eye contact between dogs is a sure sign of aggressive intent. Our mistress understood this too and barely moved her head as she watched the Chow through her eyelashes.

Miles whispered to me, "We must protect the mistress and Muffin. I'll follow your lead. Signal me and we'll go after him together."

Miles, the dog I wanted to emulate, who was my idol and my teacher, *trusted me* to make the right judgment! Miles had no experience in dogfights. Now I understood what teamwork meant. With Miles nearby, willing to help, depending on my experience, and accepting my bravery as a fact, I knew I would not let him or my mistress down.

"Maintain position," I whispered back. "If he tries anything, you bite his hind legs. Try to break his bones. I'll go for his throat. If that doesn't drive him off, pull hard on his legs so he falls over and I will aim for his gut."

Throat or underbelly contact was serious. Amateurs bite anything they can reach. True dog-dog confrontations result in heavy damage to throats, necks and the vital organs of the stomach area.

The Chow could kill Muffin with one bite and a shake. Our mistress could not bite and stood on only two legs. It would be easy for the Chow to knock her over and hurt her. Four legs make physical impact harder so dogs have advantages over humans in attacks. Miles and I knew it was our responsibility to protect our mistress and Muffin.

Miles gulped fearfully but he trusted my leadership. I would not allow this thug to hurt my family! No respectable dog would attack another dog showing neutral or submissive postures, like our sitting. But the Chow had no respect. He was a big bully. He could not be trusted.

The mistress began humming softly. I did not know if she wanted to reassure us or calm the Chow. We stayed still. Birds chirped. The Chow froze into an aggressive stance, ready to pounce on the first one of us who moved. Slowly he lowered his head and silently bared his enormous teeth. A butterfly flitted close to the Chow's head. In a flash, he snapped his jaws and the butterfly disappeared. We jumped at the clash of his teeth.

The day became eerily quiet, and even the birds were silenced by the Chow's air snap. All creatures understood the threat. My hind legs went numb. The Chow moved from his frozen posture and began stalking around us in slow motion. Muffin's body was immobilized, but she timidly turned her head away to avoid the Chow's gaze. Her eyes froze, looking at the ground as if an imaginary tiny bug was the most fascinating thing in the world. We waited for the Chow to attack.

Then, far away, a man's voice yelled. He called a name and whistled. The Chow's ears moved but he continued staring at us. The man whistled and called again. This time he sounded impatient. The Chow's lips dropped back over his teeth, like a black curtain.

"Grrrrr!" grumbled the Chow. "You're not worth my energy," he bragged. He trotted off with his arrogant head and tail in the air. His human did control him after all. I was not surprised he had lied—bullies often cover their own fear and insecurities with lies and aggressiveness towards others. His master clanged the gate after the Chow entered his own yard. With the Chow safely locked in, our mistress called to the man.

"Your dog is aggressive. He's pinned us here. You should never allow him loose off leash."

"Baloney." The man waved stiffly. "I let him run for a while to get exercise. He always comes when I call."

"Your dog is dangerous. He threatened to attack us."

The man turned away. "Mind your own business, Lady." He followed his dog into their house.

We began to breathe again.

"Free dogs." Our mistress sighed our release words.

"That was close," Miles shook himself to relieve his tension.

"I'm glad it didn't come to a fight." I stretched my hind legs to get the blood flowing again.

"You boys are a real team." Muffin shook off her fear. "I feel safe with you two." I looked sideways at her and could not believe she admitted her feelings about us—especially me! Muffin shyly looked me in the eye and instead of disdain, I saw the tiniest crinkle of a smile. I winked at her. I saw a new side to her fake toughness. I realized that sometimes little folks need to try to be bossy to protect themselves from big folks. Puddin' always shared her insecurities with me and I loved her for it. Now I found I loved Muffin for her spunkiness. She winked back. It became a silent, never talked about truce. I felt I finally, truly, belonged to everyone in this remarkable family.

"Excellent work, my puppies. Let's get out of here." The mistress led us away.

We resumed our walk but looked back frequently to make sure the Chow did not follow us. When we were a safe distance away from the Chow's yard, the mistress praised us and gave us kisses and rubs. Then she took out the little box she carried in her pocket. She pushed buttons on the phone and called the police to report the man and his dog.

"What if the Chow had come upon a child," she said into the box. "I'll file a formal complaint. He should receive a citation. No one should let a dog like that loose."

Several weeks later we were in the field behind our house. Muffin sniffed out mouse holes. I could not see her because the grass was so high but I heard her collar tags stop jingling.

"Hey, guys," she hollered. "Look over here!" Miles and I ran towards the sound of her voice. We smelled a terrible smell. The mistress followed us. We stopped at Muffin's side. The mistress moaned when she joined us.

There were the remnants of the Chow's body. His collar laid in the grass, separate from his body and torn to shreds. Even the little metal tags were bent. Parts of him were gone, bugs and flies crawled all over his remains. Our noses told us the story. Coyote scent was everywhere. We knew coyotes lived in our field and we saw them from time to time but the mistress kept us on our leashes and safe. We respected the coyotes and they left us alone.

The Chow's master had turned him loose for an unsupervised run, which was dangerous for others and for the dog. But instead of bullying people and other dogs, the Chow had stupidly challenged the coyotes. It must have been a terrible fight. The arrogant Chow never had a chance with animals as wise and wild as coyotes.

The mistress called us away. She shook her head. "Although the Chow was aggressive, no domestic dog deserves such a death. It is the responsibility of humans to protect their dogs. I'm mad at the man who allowed his dog to be killed."

I did not like the Chow but regretted that he died. I had never seen a dead animal before. Finally I understood what death was. Would this happen to me? Would my body end up in a field with bugs all over it? Whatever death was, it scared me.

Chapter 16

Visiting

We spent four years going to classes, shows, and all kinds of functions with people and their dogs. I learned that dogs could be nice and people kind. I grew into new depths of love for Miles, Muffin, the cats, and most of all, my mistress. I finally knew where I belonged and I was loved for myself. I won many ribbons and titles to show how special I had become.

We also went to places to cheer up sick people. I learned to be gentle and not afraid of wheelchairs, canes, machines that made noise, and strong, disagreeable smells. My first time in an old folks' home I walked between Miles and the mistress. The narrow halls smelled of bleach, which made me sneeze. I felt claustrophobic and nervous.

Along the hallways old men and women sat in wheelchairs, shuffled by with walkers, or were rolled on beds with wheels. I did not want to knock anybody down or get hit with the wheels so I tucked my head against Miles' flank. When we arrived in the meeting room rows of old people in wheelchairs were circled around our performance area. We no sooner entered the door behind the people than we heard an old man's wavering voice shout at us.

"Shep! Shep! Come here, old boy." We turned toward an old man sitting in his wheelchair in the back of the meeting room.

"Hello, Mr. Whistler. I've brought my new dog Max this time. Isn't he a beauty?" My mistress gave me a hand signal to approach. The old man ignored her but focused his cloudy eyes on me.

"Shep, my good boy. Where you been, Buddy? You been gone too long, I almost gave up hope. You gotta realize them rabbits can run farther and faster than you." His voice crackled. Some words sounded scratchy, some were so quiet I could barely hear them. But his call for someone named "Shep" was unmistakable.

I looked at my mistress, cocked my head, pricked my ears, raised my eyebrows in question, and awaited her answer.

"I found Shep for you, Mr. Whistler." My mistress looked over Mr. Whistler's head, toward the nurses behind a long paneled desk. Their eyes had opened wide and they vigorously nodded to my mistress. They waved her to continue. The old man ignored my mistress and crooned words of affection to me. He patted me hard on the head. I usually hated when people did that but this time I patiently stood still.

The old man stroked me and his boney hand trembled all the way down my back. He weakly scratched my rear end with deformed fingers and when I looked up to smile at him his face shone wet with tears.

We shared a few more minutes with Mr. Whistler then moved to the front of the people and did our tricks. Miles opened a drawer with his mouth and dug out hidden toys, played dead after the mistress "shot" him with her finger, and took a dumbbell to an old lady's lap and dropped it. The old lady stiffly threw the dumbbell and Miles retrieved it then took it back to the lady. She giggled like a little girl.

Muffin crawled, rolled over, waved, and barked on a hand signal our mistress taught another lady. The old ladies liked Muffin because she fit in their laps.

I retrieved balls, bowed, followed my mistress without a leash, and laid my head in people's laps when the mistress told me to. All three of us did sit/stays, down/stays and came to our mistress on hand signal, just like in the dog shows. After our tricks we weaved around the wheelchairs so everyone could pet us.

When it was time to go, Mr. Whistler was asleep. His bald, splotchy head bent forward and his spotted, arthritic hands hung limp on the arms of his wheelchair. Our mistress picked up our toys and packed our equipment while nurses wheeled old folks back to their rooms. A large-boned nurse as tall as my mistress came to us.

"I can't express my appreciation to you for bringing your new dog. Mr. Whistler hasn't spoken or responded to any of us for over two years since his stroke. There's something special about Max that triggered long-ago memories for him. We didn't know he could talk." There were tears in her eyes too. She hugged my mistress and rubbed me under my chin, then kissed me on the head.

We saw Mr. Whistler every time we went to his nursing home. He always called me Shep and I went to him. One day he did not come to our show. The big-boned nurse asked if the mistress would bring me to Mr. Whistler's room because he had suffered another stroke. When we got to his bedside, our mistress told Miles and Muffin to down/stay. They lay in the doorway while I was allowed all the way in. The nurse pushed a chair close to Mr. Whistler's head.

"Max, paws up," my mistress patted the seat of the chair. I climbed up with my front feet and they lowered the side rail of the bed.

"Mr. Whistler, Shep's here to see you. Can

you wake up?" The nurse touched the old man's scrawny, bruised arm. He had a tube stuck in his other arm and machines hummed on that side of the bed. A clear plastic tube hooked over his ears and plugged into his nose. I heard the whoosh of air that blew into him.

I stretched my neck and laid my head on the pillow next to Mr. Whistler's ear. He smelled funny—stale, sick, sour—but his sheets smelled like bleach and his blanket like fabric softener. It was a strange combination. I ignored his odors and nudged him in the ear with my nose, then kissed his stubbly cheek lightly. His thin, stiff, white whiskers stabbed my tongue. Mr. Whistler's eyes slowly opened, blinked a few times, and he heavily rolled his face to mine.

"Shep," he whispered tenderly. "Shep, my best buddy. Chase any rabbits today? I knew you'd come back to me." He tried to raise his hand to pet me but it only came a few inches off the blanket, quivered, then dropped back down at his side. I gently placed my paw over his arm to let him know it was okay if he could not pet me. He smiled weakly, drew a deep breath, sighed it out, and moaned contentedly. He gazed into my eyes lovingly, and still looked at me when his eyelids closed again. His face relaxed but the tiniest smile remained. We quietly left him and went home.

The next morning the phone rang. After talking for a short while, my mistress hung up then sat on the floor and hugged my shoulders. "You are a wonderful, special dog, Max. Mr. Whistler died last night. His last memory was your face, your eyes, your paw, and your kiss. The nurses wanted me to thank you for making his last hours peaceful. He never woke up after you left his side."

I did not know people died too. Where did Mr. Whistler go? Was he afraid to die, like me? Or was he brave like Butch had been?

Chapter 17

Home Life

In the winters Miles and I chased each other around the yard and wrestled in the snow. Miles was constantly drenched because he was always on the bottom. I was "top dog" and remained dry. I was bigger than him too, so whenever he tried to get out from under me, I just flopped down and pinned him. When we went into the house the mistress laughed at us. Miles was always a good sport and we had a great time being brothers. Although I continued to admire Miles, I felt more like an equal friend than a worshipping subordinate.

After the confrontation with the Chow, Muffin seemed to like me more. We maintained a silent truce. Sometimes she acted like the boss and sometimes I did. If she knew more about something, I followed her and learned. If

I proved more knowledgeable, she let me lead. Muffin taught me how to play without hurting her. She liked to hide under the couch and bark at me. When I tried to get her she darted out from under the couch, nipped me on my front toes, and yipped, "Gottcha!" Then she dove back in. I could not pay her back because I was too big to get under the couch.

Muffin and I also played tug-of-war with toys but I tried to be careful how hard I pulled. She was little but did not see herself as a small dog. And she had one colossal personality. She was extremely competitive so many times I swallowed my own ego and let her win. Other times I just dragged her—she stubbornly would not let go of our tug rope. But our times together became fun, not antagonistic.

Murphy the cat shook her head because she thought we were dumb. Mariah curled up on the other side of the room in a chair to watch us, and Sheba giggled. Although Sheba could not see us, Muffin's squeals and my grunts of frustration entertained her.

Before bedtime, Miles, Muffin, and I laid side-by-side chewing on bones. We were like real siblings. Inside, in front of a fireplace with a family at last, I still felt my good fortune was an unreal dream. The cats slept on the back of the couch or in our mistress' lap. Our parakeets chirped gleefully all day until they were covered up for the evening when we all went to bed.

I no longer had to sleep in the crate but had my own room and my own bed. Even though the mistress let me sleep upstairs with the others, I decided to sleep in the sunroom year round because there were lots of windows to look out and it was not heated. I had thick fur that made me too hot in the house and I liked watching the outdoor critters in the early mornings. But knowing I was welcome everywhere made me feel like part of the family I had always dreamed of.

Instead of being afraid when I was alone, I learned aloneness did not mean loneliness. I eventually relished my private time, knowing my family was near but that I was free to be by myself if I wanted to be. I loved our dog door because I could go outside and sleep in the sun or explore the yard by myself. I knew that if I needed company I could always go back inside.

The more included I was in this family, the more confident I became and therefore, the less needy to have someone always around. I also learned to respect the others' needs for downtime away from the rest of us. Mariah especially spent time off by herself, but we all had opportunities to spend time alone. If my mistress left, I no longer panicked about her return. I became comfortable in my own skin and with my own thoughts.

During warm summer nights everyone slept downstairs with me in the sunroom. We looked out at night on our yard, the field, and the starry sky over our trees. In the mornings we watched the sun rise beyond the horizon and heard the outside wild birds awaken. In the afternoons Miles, Muffin, our mistress, and I spent time together in our yard, while the cats and parakeets watched us from the sunroom windows.

Murphy, Mariah, and Sheba were not allowed outside because animals like coyotes, raccoons, and skunks visited. They might have enjoyed a *cat steak* so the mistress kept our cats safe inside the house with the parakeets. The parakeets enjoyed watching their wild cousins at the feeders in the trees and squawked at splashes the wild ones made in the birdbaths.

On those magical summer nights we all jumped into bed with the mistress. I felt peace and love at last. It was not the same as my mother's love but it was good for a grown-up dog. I no longer startled at new sounds, and when I slept, it was at night because I knew I was safe. I rarely thought about abandonment or death anymore. I lived each moment joyfully, warm in the arms of my mistress, and in the accepting company of my animal family.

Chapter 18

Mariah

The cats got used to me after I first met them, and although I could be clumsy, they rubbed around my legs and purred at me. Mariah became my favorite. A big orange, black, and white tortoiseshell-patterned cat, Mariah did not care for dogs or other cats but she loved me.

We walked around the house with her between my front legs. I loved her tail tickling my tummy. When we lay on the floor Mariah cuddled under me, her head stuck out of my ruff fur, and the rest of her invisible under my chest between my front legs. I was careful not to squish her.

Mariah and I learned to communicate the same way I learned to understand our mistress. Cats verbalize more than dogs and use a variety of chirps, mews, and yowls. But they also communicate with body language and many of their movements mean the same in dog language.

Cats also use their tails more than dogs to communicate. I knew Mariah's moods by watching her tail. Each time she saw me, her tail made wide, high swooping sweeps in greeting. If she was annoyed, just the tip slapped up and down. When she grew curious, her tail hung low and straight, and when she felt playful, her whole tail whipped up and down and back and forth.

Mariah and I were laying by the patio door watching birds and squirrels at the feeders outside when she turned to me and laid her front paw over mine. I looked down at her and smiled. I thought she wanted to share something but I also knew how private she was. She had learned to trust me and shared more about her life little by little.

"My mother left us kittens. I don't know what happened to her, but one day she went hunting and never came back. We lived in rocks in a field near some houses. My littermates and I waited for our mother to return and feed us. We got hungrier and hungrier. That night we shivered without our mother to keep us warm. We cried for her.

"Some human teenagers found us and put us in a box then dropped us into a smelly metal dumpster. The sun had just risen the next day when we heard a roar from a big motor. The ground, the dumpster, and our box vibrated from the noise. We cried louder and louder for our mother to protect us.

"She didn't come but a man in a gray uniform looked over the high edge of the dumpster, saw us in the box, yelled, and the motor stopped. The ground became still and quiet. I saw the man's head peer over the top of the dumpster again. Then a second man looked over too.

"'Here we go again.' the first man said. 'More kittens disposed of in the trash.' The man heaved his bulky leg over the lip of the dumpster and clambered into the stinky mess of garbage, papers, and bags. He wrapped his dirty, big, gloved hands around our box and pushed us up to the edge. The second man took our box from him and held us while the first man climbed out. The man who held us was dirty too. He was short and skinny and had a nice smile. They both smelled like rotten food.

"'Nice kitty, kitty, kitties,' the skinny man said. 'No need to be scart no more. I got ya.'

"'It makes me mad that people are so heartless,' the first man dropped from the top of the dumpster and dusted his uniform off with sooty gloves. 'If sumbody didn't want them kittens, why didn't they take 'em to a shelter where they coulda been fed and cared for? Them places find 'em homes then. It breaks ma heart when they leave such young uns to be kilt in such scary ways like leavin' 'em in garbage dumpsters. No animal deserves to be scart. Come on, Slats, let's take 'em to the shelter. They look pretty cold and hungry.'

"'But, Fred, what if the boss finds out we missed a hour of work?' Slats' smile disappeared.

"'What else we gonna do with 'em? We cain't keep 'em in a hot truck all day. If the boss don't like it, we just tell him it was the right thing to do.'"

Mariah continued, "We were taken in at the shelter and put together in an enclosure with other kittens. We got food and milk and had toys. That's where our mistress found me. She wanted a companion for Murphy.

"Murphy's too bossy. She likes Miles more than me. When we sleep with the mistress, Murphy sleeps under the covers cuddled with the mistress and makes me stay at the foot of the bed. If I try to cuddle with the mistress, Murphy bats me with her front paws. I don't think Muffin likes me either. So I stick to myself. Sheba came after me and follows Murphy like a kitten follows a queen cat. At least I have food and a nice place to live.

"Then you came. You were like me. You were so sad when you came. I felt we could be good friends and I wanted to help you become happy. Even though you were a big klutz, I saw you needed love. I'm glad you're here."

One day when the mistress was gone Mariah played on a table. None of us were supposed to get on tables but Mariah liked to be naughty. Somehow the tag on her collar got caught in a crack and she could not get her head free. She got mad and started to pull and wiggle around. She fell off the table and could not get back up. Murphy jumped onto the table to comfort Mariah but could not help. Murphy called for me but I did not know what to do.

Desperately I looked all around to see if there was something, anything, that would stop the nightmare of Mariah's little gags. What could I do? I stuck my head under Mariah's feet but her flailing claws only scratched me. I could not get her feet planted on my neck so I could push her up onto the table again. I felt utterly helpless and inadequate to save my dear friend. In a mounting panic I had never felt, I hollered for wise Miles. He ran in but we could only look at each other, realizing we were useless. Only our mistress could help but she was gone. Frightened Sheba slinked away and hid.

Mariah choked to death in front of us. None of us could do anything but be with her as her life faded away. We froze in our places, as if her death had taken our ability to move too.

It seemed like forever until our mistress came in the back door. At the same moment, we all jumped and ran to her. We got her attention immediately because we were all frantic. Miles ran around her and Muffin jumped up on her hind legs with her front paws on the mistress' legs. I bumped the mistress with my shoulder to herd her the right direction. I knew she would not hit me like my old master did when I tried to help him understand. Murphy yeowled, Miles whined, and Muffin cried.

Our mistress looked from one to the other of us and said, "What is it?" Worry built on her face as her eyebrows crinkled and her eyes darted to each animal.

I stepped forward and gave a great bark. When our mistress looked at me, I barked and barked, "This way, Mistress! Help!"

Concern flooded her face. She knew something was very wrong. She followed me into the room where Mariah hung lifeless from the table, her tag still stuck in the crack. The mistress shrieked, grabbed Mariah, freed her from the collar, and began breathing into her mouth. The room was silent, except for our mistress' breaths disappearing into Mariah. Mariah did not respond.

"No, no, no! Mariah, my sweet girl! Come back to me!" Our mistress gave up and collapsed on the floor, cuddling Mariah's limp body and rocking back and forth. Tears ran out of her eyes and fell on Mariah's beautiful fur. Her wrenching sobs echoed through the house.

None of us had ever seen such anguish in our mistress. We looked at each other confused, afraid, sad, and unsure, because our mistress was the family's steady center, the leader that kept us together. We depended on her but at that moment she fell apart.

We bunched together and watched as she wrapped Mariah's body tenderly in a soft towel and laid her on her cat bed. Her sobs were quieter but even scarier as she stomped back into the room to the table where poor Mariah's collar hung without her. The mistress grabbed Mariah's collar, yanked the tag out of the table crack and threw it against a wall.

Through her sobs our mistress screamed words we had never heard. None of us had ever heard her scream at all. We had never heard her shriek or cry. None of us had seen such anger in her. But at the same time she was heartbroken. Angry and sad at the same time. In a flash I thought of Puddin' and our discussions about how complex and unpredictable human emotions were.

We backed up and watched our mistress when she called the veterinarian's office, and as she spoke she erratically paced in circles. All of us cowered in confusion and fear. When she ended the call, she again broke down in wrenching, breathless sobs and again cradled Mariah's lifeless body in her arms.

Eventually she laid Mariah down, stroked her fur, then covered her with the towel one last time. Then the mistress went to Murphy and Sheba. Sheba had crept out and cuddled next to Murphy. Despite their anxiety, they held still as our mistress reached for Murphy first. By the time our mistress picked Murphy up, she had become gentle again, although her tears still flowed down her cheeks. We knew we could trust her hands to never hurt us. She took Murphy's and Sheba's collars off of them and threw all the cat collars in the trash. She never made the girls wear them again.

A lady from the veterinarian's office came to our house and took Mariah's body away. I never saw my cat again.

No one in the family slept much that night. If we dozed, sudden loud sobs from our mistress woke us. She tossed and turned all night—it was hard to tell if she was awake or asleep. Murphy and Sheba tried to lay beside her but had to keep moving when our mistress rolled from one side of the big bed to the other. Finally our mistress stilled, with her arms around Murphy. Murphy did not move but only purred her loud comforting purr. Sheba stayed close on the pillow next to the mistress' head. Miles and Muffin stayed in their own beds, next to the mistress' bed. I slept upstairs with everyone that night. I did not want to be alone and I wanted to be near in case my sorrowful mistress needed me. Mariah's place at the foot of the bed was empty.

I missed Mariah, my first best friend who was not a bird, dog, or person. I had never seen a group of creatures mourn together. For the first time since leaving my mother I was not alone in my despair. We tried to help each other and spent a lot of time near our mistress. We wanted her to know we loved her and appreciated her good, kind care of us.

No one could have helped Mariah. It just happened. We had never thought about the rules of our house and no one wondered why we were not allowed on tables. We were not allowed outside at night alone either. I thought about my mother's words when she taught us to obey her. I did not know that she was protecting her puppies from danger. The mistress had rules that I followed so I could stay at her house—I never thought that maybe those rules were to protect me.

I thought a lot about what one moment of naughtiness could become. Mariah was not a bad girl—just a rebellious one. I thought her mischievousness was funny, like when she snuck out our dog door and into the yard. I never thought the yard could be dangerous for her. I had to think hard about the rules I had learned and understand how each was a sign of our mistress' loving protection. The thought that my mistress was so like my mother was a revelation, a surprise, and yet a comfort. But now it was my job to comfort her.

The mistress cried often and we gathered around and tried to help her feel better. Miles leaned against her leg and I put my head in her lap. Murphy and Sheba rubbed against her and purred. Muffin brought toys and tried to get the mistress to play. It took us a long time to adjust to the loss of Mariah. I was sorry Mariah never knew how much everyone loved her. I was glad she had known I loved her as much as she loved me.

The mystery of death continued to distress me. Mariah's body had only remained in our house until the vet lady came and took her away. But even I could tell Mariah's personality had gone away. Where did the real Mariah go? Dogs died. People died. Cats died too. Where did they all go? Were they frightened? Some died because they were mean. Some were unloved. Some were neglected. Some were old and sick. Mariah was loved, young, and healthy. Yet death took her, too. It frightened me to realize death could also be accidental.

Blind and a bit nervous, our silver tabby cat Sheba, skipped around me at first because I stepped on her now and then. But she stopped running away from me when she realized Mariah trusted me. After Mariah's death Sheba often sat near me, as she used to sit near

Mariah. Mariah had told me she thought Sheba worshipped Murphy but I often saw Sheba's affection for Mariah, especially when they were near each other on the couch. After Mariah died, Sheba often lay near me on the rug in front of the fireplace. Sheba was not much of a talker and she was very shy. But she did like to listen to the rest of us chat and to be near us.

Murphy was bossy but funny. Often I climbed on our mistress' lap when she sat in her recliner chair with her legs up. I weighed sixty pounds but she let me climb up like a puppy. If Murphy had already curled on the mistress' lap, she would not move. Murphy's stubbornness made me giggle. If she refused to share the mistress' lap, I climbed on top of her. Murphy refused to give up her spot to me, even when she was squished.

If I got on our mistress' lap first, Murphy climbed up on top of me and lay on my back. So we had a sandwich of human, dog, and cat. The mistress laughed, I smiled my big grin and Murphy was careful not to stick me with her claws.

Everyone had a good time being together. Mariah's death helped us appreciate each other and realize our family time was precious. None of us could see into the future and so we lived each moment, aware and thankful for our circle of love. Even Muffin was nicer to everybody.

Chapter 19

Lifesaver Dog

Muffin put her nose in the air and squealed, "Water's up!" She ran away and her short, skinny black legs blurred in the dun-colored dust she kicked up. We had arrived at a place I had never been. We jumped out of the car and Muffin took off.

Everywhere I looked I saw dogs and people walking, running, and playing freely. We were at a reservoir near our house and it had prairie fields, woods, and ponds. Dogs did not have to be on leashes so it was a safe, fun place for everyone who loved dogs and for the dogs who were not as smart as we were off-leash.

"Come swim with us!" Miles jumped forward to chase Muffin but at the same time he looked back at me. I pricked my ears and ran after them. I had not gotten far when I realized we had left our mistress alone. I did not know what excited Miles and Muffin so much and I wanted to go see. Yet I did not want to leave my mistress alone if she would be in danger. I stopped and turned back towards her.

"Go, go! Have fun, Max. I'll be right there." She waved me off with the same hand signal she used in obedience competition. She could not run as fast as we could. Reassured, I turned and galloped after my brother and sister.

Miles and Muffin had disappeared and I thrashed through the thick shrubs following their scents. Ahead I heard voices of dogs and people. All of a sudden the ground beneath my feet disappeared. I hung for a split second in mid-air and then dropped. Something cold devoured my body. It gushed up over my head, filled my ears, blurred my eyes, and bubbled into my nose.

Instinctively my front legs began to pump, but my outstretched toes grabbed nothing but liquid. Shocked by my weightlessness, I felt my body gradually float upward until I resurfaced into the light, spitting, sputtering, and gagging on the thick wet goo stuck in my throat.

When I felt semi-solid mud under my paddling feet I stood up, gasped, and shook my head so my eyes could clear. A black blob and a little dark dot near me exploded into uproarious laughter. I immediately recognized Miles' and Muffin's voices. I shook my body and heard the scatter of water like after a bath. My vision cleared and I saw not just Miles and Muffin but several other dogs and their people.

I had blindly run off the bank of ground and landed in one of the ponds. I had only been bathed in a tub until this experience and never been completely submerged in water. No wonder I had no idea what happened to me! All the other dogs were already drenched and the ones who retrieved balls dropped them in the water to laugh at my antics.

"A dainty swan you ain't," laughed one drippy black Lab.

"Hey, klutz! Bet you can't do that again," hollered a muddy mixed breed with leaves stuck to his mucky mottled fur.

Two black female Portuguese Water Dogs huddled together, whispered and squealed with delight.

"Way to go, Graceful!" boomed a Great Dane whose fawn-colored coat had a distinct dirt line across his shoulders, belly, and flanks from wading in the murky shore water.

"Your name should be Sinking Stone, not Max," giggled Muffin.

"Are you all right?" Miles tried to control himself and show concern.

I threw back my head and laughed too. "I guess if dogs were meant to fly, we would have wings instead of tails, huh? Wait a minute," I looked at my tailless rear end, "I don't have *either!*" I joined in their mirth.

Muffin took the opportunity to steal a chocolate Lab's tennis ball that floated out of his reach. She scrambled out of the water and up the slippery embankment with it between her teeth as it dripped brown water. Our mistress emerged from the shrubs and joined everyone.

"What's so funny?" She looked around at all the people still laughing. One of the men filled her in on my attempt to fly. Then she laughed too. I loved to see her happy and wiggled my wet bottom.

Muffin scampered over and asked the mistress to throw the purloined ball for her. Muffin stood on her hind legs and pawed the air, her bug eyes pleaded, and the filthy ball protruded out of her tiny mouth. The people had a new source of entertainment. Once again competitive Muffin stole attention.

The mistress laughed again, reached down, took the ball from Muffin, and threw it far out into the pond. We all lunged for it. The ball bobbed on the wakes of dogs racing out to fetch it. One by one the dogs tired or became concerned about their distance from shore and paddled back. Eventually just Muffin and I swam nose to nose.

"Hey, I didn't know you could swim," Muffin puffed.

I didn't know I could either! My intense sense of competition against Muffin took over and I had done something I did not know I could do. But when I realized I was in very deep water for the first time, reason took over. This was a new experience and I suddenly became afraid. I paddled around and swam back to shore. I stood near Miles wheezing.

"Well, that was stupid of me!" I could hardly breathe and my legs quivered with the exertion of moving through water. I had used muscles I never used—running on dry ground was completely different.

"You and Muffin will kill each other someday with your pride and lack of awareness of anything else when you're competing." Miles laughed and shook his head.

I knew he was right. I decided I needed to keep a more level head when Muffin goaded me into doing things I should not have been doing.

When Muffin proudly returned, she courageously fought off the other dogs' attempts to snatch the ball out of her mouth. She laid it at our mistress' feet, panting for another throw.

"That's quite a Rottweiler you've got there," called one of the men who owned three mixed breed dogs of various sizes and colors. The humans laughed again. All the dogs formed a towering, drooling, staring circle around scrawny, drenched Muffin and her stolen ball. She laid back her ears, squinted her eyes, lifted her lip menacingly and said, "Just *try* it, any one of you. Finders keepers, losers weepers."

I loved swimming. I loved being weightless and free to explore water and new habitats. I could access little islands with fascinating smells, or cool my body in the heat of summer, just by swimming into deep water. The mistress taught us the words, "Go swim," and we all shot away and bounded into whatever pond was near.

By the start of autumn I could go as far as Muffin. Miles rarely swam out far. He stayed near the mistress, and watched us. When Muffin and I came in closer he and I wrestled in the stinky brown shore water.

The tree leaves had just begun to turn golden when we were invited on an autumn picnic at our reservoir by a dog club our mistress wanted to join. Many dogs and their families met at an area with tables, grills, and space for us to run. It was near our pond so we could play in the water if we got too hot. Another club member brought her three-year-old daughter, Emily. They did not have a dog yet, but the little blond girl loved dogs and had no fear of any of us.

Emily was fascinated by Muffin because she was little, like Emily was. Muffin never liked children and hid under a bush near me. Emily tottered around, looking for Muffin, and tried to entice her with a squeaky toy. Muffin rarely resisted squeakies but dreaded the child more than she wanted the toy.

"Go get the squeaky for me, Max," Muffin whispered from under the bush.

"Go get it yourself," I told her. I concentrated on a chewie.

"The brat won't pester you like she does me. I'll make it up to you."

"How? By stealing my chewie when I am dumb enough to leave it?" I had been victim of Muffin's pranks enough to know her plan. "No way, you're on your own." I continued to chew and Muffin continued to stew under the bush.

After a while, I put my nose in the air and savored the scents of hot dogs sizzling on the grill. My favorite food—hot dogs! Cooked or raw, I loved hot dogs! I closed my eyes and took deep breaths. Mixed with the smell of cooking hot dogs were the scents of the other dogs and people. Suddenly I realized Emily's scent was absent! Where had she gone that I could not smell her?

I sat up and looked around. The other dogs chewed treats, wrestled with each other, or slept. Miles snored next to our mistress' chair at the picnic table. I lifted my nose high but could not detect Emily's scent anywhere. I stood up and felt uneasy.

"What is it?" asked Muffin from under the bush.

"I can't see or smell Emily."

"Good riddance to the little pest!" Muffin's mouth began to water at the sight of my abandoned chewie.

For once I ignored our rivalry and moved around, sniffing and looking for the chubby child. I climbed the crest of a hillock of yucca plants. A rise in location should have brought me her scent on the breeze but the day had warmed and scents were scattered. Night dew kept scents anchored on the ground so early morning hours were better for tracking. The heat of that day dispersed Emily's scent and blew other scents over hers, which made finding her more difficult. I lowered my nose to the ground, trotted down the slope in a zigzag path and tried to get a stronger scent of Emily.

In the distance, I heard the sound of pebbles clattering and raised my head to look as well as smell. Then I saw her. Precariously close to the drop off I had fallen over the day I first learned to swim, Emily did not appear to realize the danger of the dark water below. I barked a warning and saw my mistress alert to my voice. I raced to Emily.

Emily was still looking for Muffin. She tripped on a rock and dropped the squeaky toy over the embankment into the water. She squatted to shimmy down the slimy slope to get it.

Years of dogs' feet had trampled the shoreline into a steep hole. I remembered how deep that water was.

When I reached Emily I placed myself between her solid little body and the drop-off. Emily was a determined miniature human, and she tried to go around me. I stepped in front of her again. She hit me on the back with her midget fist. I slammed her gently with my shoulder. Emily fell to the ground and began to cry. As she tried to get back up her muddy feet slipped over the drop-off and she tumbled into the pond. She landed on the floating squeaky toy and went under the water's surface.

Emily sank like I did that first time I fell in. I jumped off the precipice and landed under water next to her. She surfaced and flapped her short arms in and out of the water. I could hear her splashes and muffled cries while I was underwater near her. When I came up, I bit her shoulder, got a mouthful of her sweatshirt, and held her head up. Emily cried and coughed. I smelled her fear, even through the mud and water.

I tried to get a foothold on the embankment but it was too slippery and steep. I struggled to swim and tried to drag Emily with me toward the shallower shore. Emily's struggles tired me and made it hard to swim. I choked on water, my jaws ached, and my teeth felt like they might pop out of my gums. My leg muscles quivered and burned. Sludge blurred my eyesight and I could not tell what direction I was headed. Still Emily struggled, splashed, cried, and wriggled.

Suddenly I heard human shouts. I heard more splashes. I felt Emily lifted but my mouth would not let go of her.

"Max, GIVE!" commanded my mistress' voice. I relaxed my aching jaw and gave Emily up to the hands that reached for her. I fell back into the water still unable to see, and went under again. With my last ounce of strength, I held my breath in the murky darkness.

Then I felt arms go around me. I was lifted into the light again. Near my head, my mistress wrapped her arms around my chest, and one of the men held my exhausted rear legs under my belly. They carried me to the shallow shore and laid me down to catch my breath.

Slowly, my mind began to function. Everything I had done had been motivated by instinct. I did not plan what I did. The possibility of my own danger had not occurred to me or had a chance to frighten me. I sat up, suddenly conscious that I had *defied* death. Maybe there *was* some control over it.

"Oh Max, my brave, *special* boy!" My mistress pulled mud clots out of my mouth and wiped my caked eyes with her wet shirt. Miles licked my head and Muffin stood nearby. My chewie was in her mouth but her eyes were filled with concern.

Emily's parents took her to a hospital but she had no injury except a bruise on her shoulder where I had grabbed her.

Several days after I saved Emily my mistress took just me to a big building called a police station. It was filled with people who wore funny black uniforms and drove cars with colored lights on top. They looked like the man in black who came to my second home. It turned out they were nice people. They gave me an award. Emily and her family were there too.

Emily hit me in the head the first time she saw me after we almost drowned together. She was probably still mad because I knocked her down to keep her from falling into the water. Her mother and father scolded her for being mean to me. Newspaper reporters were there too and took pictures while Emily and I stood next to each other. They told her to kiss me and took more pictures of us. I kissed her back. Emily got a lot of attention, so she stopped being angry at me. Then we were friends.

After we joined the dog club, Emily ignored Muffin and always ran to me. Muffin laughed every time Emily hugged me so tight I could barely breathe. When Emily's fingers tangled and tugged my fur, Muffin rolled in hysterics. I could not escape Emily. Unfortunately, I was too big to hide under bushes like Muffin did.

Chapter 20

Sick Dog

"Your sixth birthday should be sometime soon, Max," my mistress said. "We'll plan a family party. But first, let's make you handsome." She went to a drawer and pulled out my favorite brush. I loved our time together when my mistress groomed me. She slid the brush through my silky fur with her right hand, then she ran her left hand gently over the same path. I leaned into her affectionately. She combed under my ears to get the knots out where my collar rubbed.

All of a sudden I felt a sharp pain, almost like the shock from the nasty collar my old master put on me. I jumped and cried. Before I could stop myself, I growled. My mistress looked worried.

"What's wrong? I didn't mean to hurt you. Hold still and let me see what it is." I licked her hand, begging forgiveness for my growl. She carefully fingered the area on my neck that hurt. Even her soft touch hurt and I cried again. "There's a little bump here," she said. "Let me take a look at it." She parted my ruff fur and squeezed the lump.

"There's no scab or hole so it doesn't look like a puncture wound. It's almost perfectly round but the hair growing out of it looks healthy. Does this hurt?" My mistress lightly pinched the perimeter of the bulge and I winced because it hurt, but I did not pull away. "Well, my boy, we're not going to guess about this." She got up, put the brush on the counter, and made a phone call.

The next morning the mistress took only me in the car. We went to the veterinarian's. I had never been there alone, usually Muffin and Miles went too. The people in white coats did things to me with needles and tubes. Then we returned home and my mistress gave me my favorite treat—stinky hot dog pieces! Hot dogs were always my treat for being a good boy. I did not know what I had done to deserve them but I was not going to turn any treat down!

Several days later my mistress and I returned to the doctor's. We went into a back room I had never seen before where I sat on a metal table and she stroked me.

"You're going to take a nap now, Max. I'll be here when you wake up. Don't be afraid, I won't leave you." I licked her hand. They poked me with something sharp and I got sleepy. My mistress scratched my tummy as I felt my front legs collapse onto the table. Scratches on my tummy always relaxed me and I drifted away listening to my mistress' loving voice.

When I woke up my neck really hurt! I forced my eyes open but the room looked blurry. My mistress sat at my side and I was lying on some blankets on a floor. As I became more awake she helped me sit up next to her. Something was different. I had a deep ache in my neck where the lump had been. They had shaved my ruff fur on my neck and I felt cool air on my exposed skin. There were two plastic tubes that stuck out of my neck. The mistress called them drains.

"You had an operation to fix the bump. It's gone now. Go back to sleep, my brave boy." I vaguely remembered the hospital technicians carrying me to our car. I did not have the strength to sit up and look out the windows so I slept all the way home.

We parked in our garage and my mistress helped me out of the car. She steadied me with a towel under my belly as I wobbled into the house. I barely made it to my bed when my legs gave out. My neck ached and I felt woozy. My animal family gathered around me.

"Welcome home, Max." Miles laid next to me on the floor near my bed.

"You stink again," Muffin whispered close to my ear.

I heard the purrs of our cats as they tiptoed around me, sniffing and nudging. Their whispers lulled me back into a dreamless slumber.

I had to take medicine hidden in hot dogs for many days after my surgery. I think the mistress thought I would not notice but I knew the medicine was there. There was still no way I could resist those stinky, delicious morsels.

Several evenings later everyone was in the family room, and I dozed on the carpet next to Miles. The mistress stretched out on the couch and watched television. All the other animals were asleep in their favorite places. The parakeets were quiet too.

Suddenly I awoke with a terrible headache. I had been sleeping a lot and the pressure in my neck was bothersome but I tried to ignore it. This headache was different. I felt nauseated and my head pounded, ba-boom, ba-boom, ba-boom, in time with my heartbeat. I did not know what was happening so I got up and went to my mistress. When I laid my head on her shoulder she looked over at me kindly then gasped. I thought I had done something wrong but her tone of voice told me she was concerned, not angry.

"Max! Oh, my poor baby." She jumped up for her car keys.

The tinkle of the keys got Miles and Muffin excited and they bounded to the back door, groggy but ready for a car trip. Once at the door to the garage they turned towards me as I came up behind them. Their mouths dropped open. The cats lazily stretched as they woke up on the couch but when Murphy saw me she stopped purring.

Miles stepped away from the door and told me, "My goodness, your head is so swollen you look like a big-headed Bull Mastiff." He tried to sound calm but pulled back his head in compassion, while his eyes bulged with shock he could not hide.

"Whoa, you look totally *gross!*" Muffin stuck her tongue out and made a gagging noise.

"Oh my," cried Sheba, then ran upstairs. She could not see my swollen head but the tension from everyone frightened her.

"We'll be waiting here for you." Murphy raised a paw and flapped her tail against the back of the couch. Even Murphy knew the car keys' jingle meant a car trip.

Our mistress told the others, "Max and I are going away for a while. Watch the house and be good." She and I went into the garage. Everyone gathered at the back door as it closed.

"In, Max." My mistress held the back door of the car open for me. I clambered onto the seat and settled in my corner to look out the window.

I wondered where we were off to at that hour. We drove fast and the lights on other cars, the streets, and the houses we passed were blurred sparkles, then fell behind our car. I could not turn my head because of the plastic tube drains in my neck so I blinked to clear my vision. But I still could not see clearly. Everything was turning hazy. Then my eyes started to ache like my head.

It was cold that late at night, so we kept the windows up. With no scents to distract me, I had no choice but to be completely aware of the incessant pounding in my head. It seemed to be getting worse. My eyes could not focus and the lights we passed muddled together.

My mistress sang to me with made-up words, "Laddida, my brave boy, you are so special, I love you so~ laddida, we're on the go~ we'll fix your woes, then home we'll go." But it was hard to take comfort from the sound of her voice with the loud banging between my ears, inside my brain, and behind my eyes. She only stopped singing for a few minutes when she talked into the little box she carried—the tiny phone. When she stopped talking she sang again as we drove on through the night.

When we arrived at a tall building with lots of lights some men in white coats came out of a double door to help us in. They lifted me out of the back seat of the car and gently laid me on a bed with wheels, like those I saw at the old folks' home. I was glad I did not have to try to walk because I felt dizzy and weak. My mistress tucked the bed's snowy blanket around me. Swaddled tightly, I laid back with her hand still on my covered shoulder as she walked beside the men, the bed, and me. I felt kind of silly being babied, but it was nice to be the center of attention without Muffin stealing sympathy.

We rolled inside and my mistress talked to a lady at the desk. It smelled like another hospital but looked big and fancy. The ceiling was high above us, there was a large round reception desk, and a glass wall had real fish in it. I tried to watch the fish, but the water appeared hazy and they just looked like multicolored blobs bobbing around.

The desk lady told the men to put us in a little room, like the one at my regular vet's. A lady doctor came in and also gasped when she saw me. My headache pounded so badly by then she looked like a white blur with a voice. The lady doctor had a young man come in to help and they cut a hole in my skin that let infected fluid drain out. It smelled icky but my headache went away. Then the lady doctor talked to my mistress and gave her more medicines. The sun glowed in the eastern sky when we finally went home.

Three more times my mistress and I did this late night run to the emergency room. Each time my head had swollen and each time when they drained the fluid away, my headache stopped and my vision returned to normal.

Then we went to this night hospital in the day. My mistress stroked me, they poked me, and I got sleepy again. When I woke up my mistress was gone and I suffered with another burning pain in my neck. People in white coats put me into an enclosure like the one at the shelter but much smaller. I was laid on a cushiony pad with blankets that smelled like the fabric softener at the old folks' home that they wrapped Mr. Whistler in. But I did not know any of these people.

I felt so sick to my stomach I could hardly think. Did my mistress give me away? Was I too much trouble? Did she decide she did not want to take care of me? I could not go to dog shows and win ribbons when I did not feel well. The haunting trauma of homelessness returned. Was I no longer loved by the person who meant the world to me? My heart broke and my thoughts raced. I cried out loud. My own voice sounded far away and was a pitch I had never heard myself make before. I quieted and curled up in the back of the cage and tried to cuddle under the blankets.

My mind would not stay on dreams of my mother, thoughts of my sweet mistress, nor could I concentrate on the activities in the hospital. I surrendered to a dark cloud that roiled into my brain and made me inconsolably sad. It reminded me of the night before my scheduled death at the shelter. I wanted to run away but I could not make my legs work. I could not even stand up. I wallowed in my misery and whined quietly. Once again, my life had crashed into rejection, pain, and despair.

The people in white coats spent a lot of time taking care of me and all of them were kind. But I wanted my mistress. I wanted to go home. I missed my family, even Muffin! I slept a lot and did not dream at all. I could not eat and I had no interest in what went on around me. Dogs in neighboring enclosures groaned in discomfort while I moaned in my own tiny prison.

One morning a familiar scent woke me up. I felt a surge of unexplained happiness and slowly opened my eyes. Above me stood my mistress! She had returned for me! Overjoyed, I tried to get up to greet her but she sat down on the floor, put her hands on me and firmly held me still.

"Max, stay. You had an operation to fix the first one. It's more serious and you must remain in the hospital for a few days, but then I will come get you and bring you home. Everyone misses you. You're a *special*, brave dog." She smiled but she looked tired. Had she worried about me? She stayed next to me and talked to me and the people in white coats. I drifted in and out of sleep comforted by the sound of her voice.

I woke up again when I felt her stir. I tilted my head in question, raised my brown eyebrows and whined. I did not want her to move away from me. My mistress kissed my head, scratched behind my ears, and stood up.

"Visiting time is over, Max. I'm going home but I'll be back tomorrow. I love you." Then she left me again. But my mistress came every day after that, and when I grew strong enough she took me for a slow walk in the hospital exercise area. It felt wonderful being with her and my fear of her abandoning me began to fade.

I went home on a beautiful spring day and everyone gathered around me when I collapsed on the family room floor. "The house hasn't been the same without you," said Murphy. She butted her head against my shoulder and rubbed her cheek on my front paw. Her tail swished in welcome and she purred when she nosed my nose.

"I missed wrestling and running with you," said Miles. He lay down on his side next to me and gently placed his front paw on mine.

"Are you feeling better?" Even shy Sheba came downstairs. She rubbed against my back and purred too. I had never felt so loved.

"Jeesh, you stink *again!*" Muffin wrinkled her nose and made a goofy face. Muffin did not like the smell of hospitals. Then she brought me one of her favorite toys. "Here, you can play with my squeaky. But you'd better give it back when I want it." Her words were meant to sound tough but her tone was sympathetic.

"Thanks, but I'm so tired I'll play later." I flopped over on my side for a nap. I dozed but felt each cat and Miles sniff me gently. Muffin licked my face. I kept my eyes closed and tried to hide a smile—although she would never admit it, deep down Muffin cared. I wanted to jump up and cry, "See! I knew you liked me!" but I did not have the energy to tease Muffin. My mistress stroked my fur and I sighed with contentment.

My mistress and I returned to the fancy hospital one week later. We went into the first exam room with the lady doctor. Another lady doctor came in. Then another doctor, a tall man, put x-rays up on a light board on the wall. They talked in words I did not understand. Everyone was very serious. I fidgeted with discomfort on the cold metal exam table when my mistress put her arms around me and began to cry. Distracted from my own concerns, I kissed her face to clear her tears away and heard the word that made her so sad. . .

"Cancer."

Chapter 21

Caring and Concern

Weeks went by. I had a bandage around my neck all the time. My poor mistress had to change it every couple of hours, even through the night. My neck never healed and just kept draining. It smelled badly, even to me. Through it all, my family surrounded me. Muffin still tried to play with me although I know she hated my smell. Murphy and Sheba still purred and rubbed against me. Miles, in his gentle way, became my constant companion. He always looked after me.

On a chilly autumn afternoon Miles and I took turns peeing on things in the yard, and looked for rabbits to chase. Suddenly I felt a knife-sharp pain in my head. I collapsed on the prickly brown grass and far away I heard my own voice scream over and over. I shook uncontrollably and could not stop.

"Hold on!" Miles barked and ran into the house through the doggy door to alert the mistress. The next thing I knew my mistress knelt over me, covered me with a blanket, massaged my aching muscles, and sang to me.

When it all stopped, I felt drained and exhausted. "You had a seizure," my mistress told me. "We'll return to the vet as soon as you feel strong enough to stand and get into the car." I was big and she could not lift me so we waited until I could get up by myself. Then off we went again. The doctor gave her more medicines for me. They worked for a while.

When the mistress came down to my room in the middle of every night to change my bandage, she always let Miles and me out to potty. One early winter night I saw tracks in the new snow. My eyes followed the trail and I saw a raccoon skittering in the shadows at the far end of our yard. I was no longer afraid of these creatures, and I barked to protect my home. I ran after it and chased it up a tree. My voice had changed and become weaker in tone because of the tumor, but I still tried to sound threatening.

"Don't run!" Miles galloped after me. By then I stood on my hind legs and scratched on the tree trunk with my front paws. Suddenly, that horrible, sharp pain seared through my brain again. I fell off the trunk and landed in a heap on frozen tree roots in the dark. It took enormous effort to gather my feet under me and stand. I looked towards the house but it seemed miles away. I staggered toward the patio lights. The whole world was wavy and I could not tell where my feet were. Miles yelped to our mistress and she ran out of the sliding glass door, across the patio, and through the yard in her nightgown, robe, and slippers. I collapsed in the snow before she reached me.

I do not know how long I was unconscious. My mistress' sweet voice was singing softly when I awoke on the hard ground. Her tune teased my brain slowly back into reality, where she and Miles were at my side. A warm blanket covered me and as she sang, my mistress massaged my shoulders, back, and legs. I lifted my head and looked up at their concerned faces. Over their heads sparkling stars peeked through the naked tree branches and a strange peacefulness surrounded me. My eyes rolled in my head and I thought I saw a silent, dark shape high in that tree. Greenish orbs blinked. Then the orbs disappeared. Perhaps they were just stars. I felt confused and sick in my stomach.

I rolled onto my belly and tried to make my legs work. My mistress put her arms under my chest to help me stand. She rolled the blanket into a long strip and slid it under my hips. She lifted my body with the blanket sling and I weakly wobbled back to the house with my mistress' help. She tucked me into bed once we were inside.

Miles said, "I'll stay here with you. If you need me, just whimper and I'll wake the mistress." Usually Muffin never came downstairs after bedtime. She was afraid of the yard at night. But when she heard the commotion as we came inside that night, she did come down to my room. She tiptoed over to me and quietly laid a ball next to my bed. I slept without dreams the rest of the night.

The tumor on my neck grew into a raw, weepy bulge. The bandages my mistress invented kept the tumor covered from sight and absorbed the discharge. The smell repulsed everybody, especially Muffin, yet everyone was kind to me. My mistress spread medicine with painkillers over the mass so the pain cooled for a while.

Some days I felt like my old self and tried to play fetch. But my mistress only rolled my green tennis ball, she never threw it. She said I could not run anymore. Most of the time I was too tired to run anyway. Miles meandered slowly on our walks so I would not feel I held him back. We went shorter and shorter distances because fatigue would suddenly hit me. Then came the time when I did not have the energy to go for walks at all.

Muffin continued to offer her toys and lay next to me at night while we chewed our bones. The bump on my neck grew inside my throat now making a lump in my throat that made it difficult to swallow.

Once I did not chew a piece of my treat small enough. When I tried to swallow, it got stuck in my throat. I could not breathe. I waggled my tongue to loosen it but the wedge did not budge. I stood but fell back down again. Once more I tried to stand and walk to my mistress for help. Lack of oxygen made my head swim and spots throbbed in my eyes. I hit the floor with a thud. My mistress turned her head from where she held Murphy in her lap in the recliner chair.

"Oh! Max, what is it?" The mistress flew to me, while poor Murphy was jerked awake and plopped on the chair cushion. My mistress opened my mouth and pried out the chewie piece with her finger. I gasped for air and realized my mistress had saved my life. How could I have thought she would reject me? Even though I smelled, was sick, and could not win any more ribbons, my mistress remained devoted to me. Overwhelming relief made me dizzy again.

"That's it, my boy. No more chewies for you." My mistress shook her finger at me in fake firmness. "From now on you just get soft, squishy things to eat. I'm sorry."

My mistress' eyebrows wrinkled and we both knew something else had ended. I could no longer chew bones. I could not run or fetch balls. I could not take walks. I was no longer a show dog. I could not work anymore to earn my keep.

I kissed my mistress' cheek to let her know everything was okay as long as she stayed near me. For all the losses I faced none mattered because I finally realized the extent of her love for me. All dogs understand the desire to love and please humans but only a few humans understand how to recognize or return it. I was one of the lucky dogs that had such a person.

I missed the things I used to be able to do but I got special food now, really tasty, stinky, canned food instead of dull dry kibble. It was a special cancer diet. The canned food was easier to swallow, tasted great, and just the smell made my mouth water. I actually developed a potbelly for the first time since my puppyhood.

Chapter 22

Christmas Time

I watched my mistress put up the Christmas tree while I lay peacefully on the living room carpet one evening. Miles slept in the family room in front of the fireplace and Muffin slumbered curled up into a ball in one of the cat beds behind the door to my sunroom. Our cats were scattered around the house asleep and the parakeets napped in their cage. Only my mistress and I were in the living room listening to Christmas music while she opened box after box of ornaments and strings of lights.

My mistress put an emptied box on the floor, looked at me, and her eyes filled with tears. She came and sat next to me on the floor. She stroked me and told me something I was not sure I understood.

"Sweet Max, the end of your life with us is near. I have loved you in ways I never knew were possible. I'm proud of what kind of dog you've become. You taught me about life and how to live each moment. Every hour with you is a gift and I'm grateful you fell into our family. I am so sorry you are sick and I can't do anything to make it go away. I know you're in constant pain and you must tell me when you've had enough. When you're too tired to deal with the pain anymore, give me a sign and I will let you go."

Go where? I cocked my head, raised my eyebrows and wrinkled my forehead. I gazed at her with curiosity.

"There is a wonderful place where all animals go and some people. Only the very best are allowed in." I pricked my ears towards her voice and tilted my head in attention. I wondered if the mean neighbor dog, the Doberman who attacked me at the shelter, and the Chow would be there. I did not want to see them again.

My mistress seemed to read my mind and said, "Bad dogs get to go there because it is people who make them mean by mistreating them or breeding them poorly. You'll see your cat Mariah there. There is no illness or pain there, only happiness and fun. Some people call the place Heaven. Heaven is a perfect place for dogs and cats and you'll like it. I want you to wait there for me and the rest of our family. We'll be separated for a while but be patient, we'll be re-united someday and never be parted again."

I tried hard to understand.

"But you have to be the one to say when it's time for you to go. I don't want to see you suffer more than you can bear. Please give me a clear sign when you're ready."

What kind of sign could I give her? How would I know when I was ready? Heaven might be a wonderful place but I did not want to leave my family.

I tired easily but enjoyed looking at the lights on the inside tree. We were never allowed to pee on the inside tree but it was pretty to look at so I did not care. Some of the lights blinked off and on, while others stayed bright. The ornaments reflected the lights and sparkled. Sometimes I thought I saw faces in the reflections on the ornaments. Every face smiled at me and I felt a warmth of welcome in each vision. There were friendly faces of dogs, cats and people, but I did not recognize them.

Then I drifted off to sleep and dreamed of peeing on trees outside with Miles. I dreamed about wrestling in the snow and running in the field. I dreamed of playing tug with Muffin and cuddling with Mariah. I dreamed of Murphy lying on top of me on top of the mistress' lap. I even dreamed of shy Sheba and heard the parakeets chirping in my slumber. Sometimes the parakeets sounded a bit like Snatch. I remembered the other foster dogs whom the mistress found homes for. Memories of Puddin', Butch, my friends at the shelter, and even Mr. Whistler at the old folks' home drifted through my dreams. Sometimes I thought I saw my mother standing in fog, whining for me to join her.

Smells from the kitchen or my mistress' voice often woke me up. The activities in my home comforted me and I relaxed listening to the cats meow and purr, Muffin whine for treats, and Miles' feet softly padding nearby as he checked on me. My mistress' singing around the house or conversations with our family lulled me back into dreams of my mother. I drifted in and out of dreams and reality with equal ease. My mind was peaceful, I had no fear, no anxiety, and felt only the protective cocoon of my home. I loved each member of my family and I never wanted to "go" anywhere else.

Chapter 23

Time To Go

I slept more often, deeper, and for longer times. The house was warm and quiet. Familiar sounds of my family continued around me and delicious smells still wafted from the kitchen at mealtimes. I suffered pain but the mistress gave me medicines that helped—at least I was still allowed to eat slimy hot dogs.

I noticed my mistress had to change my bandage more often. Her gentle touch during those times of medical attention warmed my heart as the fireplace warmed my body. Our private times together as she unwrapped, cleansed, and rewrapped my neck tumor completely overpowered any of my memories of abuse, neglect, or cruelty from my past. Her final stroke when she finished always made me sleepy again.

I lost track of days and nights and often things seemed muddled together. Sometimes I went to sleep in warm sunlight but awoke in the soft lighting of lamps. If I awoke in the dark middle of the night, I could hear Miles' soft snoring nearby. He never left me unless our mistress was close. He knew my voice was gone and I could no longer call out if I needed help or if the pain peaked and it was time for more medicine.

I refused to whine for attention because I knew my mistress worried enough. I fought the pain, even when it jerked my muscles and took away my ability to control my own body. Like the emotional pain of my former loneliness, I refused to give into the physical pain of cancer. Instead I focused on all the wonderful gifts I had experienced in my life. I tried to gather all the lessons the bad times had taught me and appreciate how those lessons prepared me for the joy I eventually found. I knew I was a lucky, lucky dog.

I now had a fluffy big bed in the family room in front of the fireplace. For some reason the cancer made me always feel cold, so the sunroom windows chilled me. Inside the house, toasty, safe, well fed, and attended to, I slept almost all the time that sixth winter of my life.

During my slumbers, I spent less time in our house and more time in surreal dreams of my mother standing in grayish-white fog. She seemed to float closer and closer to me. In each dream, I tried to call to her, but no sound came out of my throat. The cancer had taken my voice in dreams, just as it had in reality. I heard Mother whine but her words echoed over each other and I could not understand her. I felt frustrated and strained to hear but then household sounds became louder and I awoke again, lying amidst my family moving around me.

Then I had a new dream. In it, the fog became brighter and I saw Mariah behind my mother! I heard her mew in her flirtatious way. Where had she come from?

The dream popped in a poof when I felt myself picked up. I smelled the scents of my mistress and her brother. Still I could not fully awaken. His strong arms lifted me and then set me down on a soft pillow. I felt a thick blanket being tucked around my body and I enjoyed the warmth. I heard the roar of a big motor. I did not recognize the sound, it was not our car. My mistress sang and stroked me. Her melodic tune comforted me and I fell into a deep sleep once again with my head in her lap and her scratches on my tummy under the blanket that was tight around me.

I drifted into more dreams of my mother and Mariah. We stood across from each other in a place of nothingness. Fog swirled and curled around us but no wind moved it and there were no trees, grass, hills, or earthly views. There did not seem to be any ground beneath our feet but Mother and Mariah stood looking at me, together and with love. They called in unison for me to join them.

I wondered how my mother knew Mariah. Mother whined and Mariah chirped to me. I froze in place. I could not make my legs walk toward them. Behind me I heard my mistress' soft voice still singing, so I turned to the sound of her melody and began to awaken.

Then I smelled that hospital smell again. I opened my eyes and forced myself into reality.

Blurry forms moved quietly around me. Were they floating? My mistress held me on a rug on a cold linoleum floor and one of those people in the white coats stabbed something sharp into my hind leg. I groggily growled at the stranger who hurt me and tried to get up.

I felt my mistress' arms tighten around me. "Relax, Max, my boy. It's time for you to go. You have been brave and patient. You've been a wonderful companion. I can't imagine my life without you but you must go. You've made me proud and I will always love you. Remember, we'll be together again. Go to sleep, my tired, brave boy. It's time to rest."

I laid back into her arms and felt her heartbeat against my shoulder. I relaxed my head in the crook of her arm. I felt the warmth of her body against my back and the coolness of the floor on my hips and hind legs. I never could fit completely in her lap.

I felt a warm rush, like water, flow from my hind leg where they stuck me. It rolled up my leg, into my hip, down my other hind leg, and then into my lower back. It slowed but continued to seep into my belly, my chest, and finally my neck. The pain melted away.

Memories flooded my brain, quickly at first and then they slowed. Was I asleep again? My mistress had saved me from the abuse and neglect that other humans inflicted upon me before we met. She rescued me from cruelty and death. Her tolerant, kind treatment helped me reclaim my battered spirit, tattered trust, and recover from my physical injuries. I had become her devoted companion and protector. My whole purpose in life was to please her.

The only peace I knew before my mistress was when I cuddled with my mother so many years ago. How many times during mistreatment and loneliness had I wondered about my mother—her whereabouts, if she was well and luckier than I?

When I became sick my mistress nursed me and never left my side. I trusted her. She would never allow anyone to hurt me. I had gotten all I desired and worked for. All my dreams came true and all my goals in my life were reached. I was loved for myself, respected for my accomplishments, and accepted as a creature who deserved kindness. I learned to trust and how to be trustworthy. I had an interesting life with work to do and friends of many species. Most of all, I found my special person, my mistress. I understood the profound and deep attachment all dogs are designed for and capable of.

"I love you, Max, my special, special boy. Godspeed you on your journey." My mistress' voice quivered. Tiny teardrops plopped on my head and I twitched my ears at the tickle. I struggled to look up at my mistress once again to see what troubled her. She smiled, stroked my face and kissed my nose. Reassured, I laid my head on her arm, kissed her hand to comfort her and to thank her for all she had done for me.

Then I floated away on a tranquil wave of untroubled peacefulness as the heat arrived in my brain. I felt my entire body go limp in my mistress' arms. Yet I could still hear my mistress' voice. She told me she loved me. . .for me to wait for her. . .how *special* I was. . .

Chapter 24

Mysterious Journey

My cancer pain bubbled to the surface of my skin and raised goose bumps. Then a rush of euphoria melted my torment away, like snow that turned to water and dripped out of the bottom of my feet. My muscles loosened from the uncontrolled spasms that had ruled my body. At last a unique quiet flowed through my back, my legs, and my neck. I submitted to the serenity that washed over my exhausted body. My last physical memory of my mistress, my feeble attempt to kiss her hand in gratitude, will remain in my mind forever. . . I had no way to know it was a kiss goodbye.

Suddenly I could not feel my mistress' arms or hear her reassuring voice. My eyes popped open and I found myself alone in a dark void. I looked for my mistress but saw only blackness. I had always been afraid of the night, and this place was darker than any night I had ever known. Panic crept into my consciousness, squeezed my brain, knotted my stomach and made my heart pound until my chest felt it would burst open. I gasped for air but had no sensation of oxygen in my lungs. Was I underwater again? No, I could breathe, but the sweetness of fresh air was absent.

Where was my mistress? I could deal with anything frightening with my mistress near but all alone in the dark I felt anxiety tearing at my courage. Then I realized I had no choice but to wait to see what would happen.

Slowly, I felt myself begin to tumble, head over feet. I somersaulted slowly at first, then faster. I began to roll from one side to the other. Nausea churned in my stomach. My body rebelled against my weightlessness—my legs and torso twisting, turning, and trying to straighten by instinct alone. My feet splayed and poked into nothingness.

Then the rolling stopped as slowly as it began. I felt my eyes strain to see anything that might indicate which way was up or down, but I could not. How did I get here? How could I get out of this nightmare and back to the comforting dreams of my mother? Or the safe embrace of my mistress' arms?

Deep within my gut arose something that had to get out. Up it climbed from my stomach to my chest, into my throat, then gurgled bitterly on the back of my tongue. I opened my mouth with an automatic retch but instead of vomit, a screech exited my body—a primitive howl I had never heard myself utter. The scream echoed ahead of me and magically opened a dim tunnel through the blackness. I felt my body sucked into the cavern.

Once in the dark circular cylinder of space, my flight evened and my body straightened. I felt right-side up. Although I made no voluntary effort to move my legs, I continued forward.

The supernatural pull sucked me faster and faster through the tunnel. There was no way to tell if I was falling down a hole or flying horizontally through a pipe. I tucked my legs under my chest and belly, laid my ears back, and lowered my head as I flew.

I emerged from the tunnel's obscure darkness into the dark gray-black fog I had dreamed of when I slept at my home. Familiar and yet strange, it seemed real but I had only seen it in dreams before. *Of course*! I understood. I was dreaming!

Relief calmed my panic. "I must be asleep," I thought. "I will awaken soon to the sound of my mistress' loving voice." I relaxed, unfolded my legs, and waited for wakefulness, for the dream to dissipate, and for reality to shine through my confusion. I waited to see my mistress' bright eyes and loving smile.

Instead, nothing changed. I traveled farther into the thick, dull fog. Disappointed and again frightened, I realized this was not another dream. The fog rolled around me and its moisture made my fur stick to my skin. I felt neither chill nor heat, no wind, and no sunshine peeked through. My feet dangled in midair, but I did not fall down. I kept going forward. No sound reached my ears—no human voices or dog barks, no hum of traffic. I stuck my head out and sniffed but not one scent penetrated my nose. I had never been anywhere that sounds and smells were completely absent. Where was I? Would I be alone forever?

Unexpectedly, I felt myself stop. I hung in the nothingness. I floated and whined. I cried as all the loneliness of my early years crashed back into my mind. Why was I being filled with sad memories? Tears slipped out of my eyes, slid down my whiskers, then disappeared in tiny flashes when they fell from my face. The sudden sparks startled me. I had never seen tears turn into sparks, although I had cried many times before. What was this place?

I sniffed and waited while I hung suspended. Time seemed nonexistent and complete silence surrounded me. Besides the churning fog I had nothing to see except the silvery tear-lights as they exploded around my cheeks. I felt sad, lonely, and scared. Sobs again heaved up from my chest, yet my wails sounded dull and the density of the mist quickly absorbed them.

Suddenly I saw a pinprick of white light far away. Stirred by curiosity and hope, I began to move my legs until I felt like I was running, but my feet never touched anything solid. Usually I heard the clicks of my toenails on dirt or pavement but here my feet were silent and my footpads remained in midair.

The fog gradually faded away in ever-lightening shades of gray, and parted in my wake like dirty water at the pond when Muffin and I chased floating balls. The light grew larger as I drew closer so I must have been going forward even though I felt no sensation of movement.

The light had a pulsating rhythm, like my mistress' heartbeat. I remembered leaning into her the last time I went to sleep, with my shoulder against her chest. But she was no longer with me. With each heart-like beat, lightning strikes pumped out from the center of the white spot. The brilliancy of the sun-like glow forced me to I squint, although I still tried to see ahead.

An itsy black spot appeared in the center of the white light. I tried to focus on it but with my eyes half closed against the shine, I could not discern a distinct form. I rotated my head from side to side and hoped to find an angle that shaded my view. The spot grew bigger and took on shape as I got closer. I could make out a head, a back, and four legs.

Two ears on top of the head pricked forward and the form's legs began to prance up and down. Gray, black, copper, and white colors on the body became visible. It twisted and wiggled, as though it was excited to see me come through the mists. I blinked back tears of relief and tried to open my eyes wider.

I was not alone! At least one other being existed—perhaps there were others in this mysterious place. I tried to run faster, before the bouncy form disappeared. Would it wait for me? What kind of being could it be? I panted from exertion and desperation. I wanted to get there before it ran away without me.

When I was close enough to see the dancer in the light, my heart flip-flopped and I gasped. My legs turned to mush and stopped all movement. I gulped in disbelief. My mouth fell open. Did I see what I thought I saw?

There in the brightness, the prancing form became. . . *my mother!*

Overjoyed, I struck out with renewed determination and stretched myself into full, strong strides. My legs propelled my weightless body until my muscles burned. Afraid I would lose sight of my mother, I raced on. The dazzling intensity of light reflected through my tears of happiness but did not blind me. When I got nearer, I saw the pulsating glow had engulfed me. I no longer needed to squint. There was a rainbow of colors, and each color shot beams out from the center source. Blues, violets, pinks, reds, yellows, and greens blended and separated as each pump of light left the vortex.

Mesmerized by the bright spectacle, I stopped running. I had never seen colors so defined and stood momentarily transfixed. Then I snapped out of my hypnosis and again searched the air for scent, sound, or any familiar sensation. But there was nothing I could identify except the form of the spirit dog, my long-lost mother.

A cloud-like, cream-colored aura surrounded my mother as she stood in front of the rhythmic glow. Joy had replaced the worry and sadness I had last seen on her face when the people took me away from her so long ago. She looked peaceful, contented, and thrilled to see me. My mother lifted her powder white right front paw in a half wave, smiled and nodded. Her blue eyes sparkled and her perfect pink tongue whipped the air as she tried to catch my scent. She stood on what appeared to be solid ground, although I had never seen such soil. Under her feet millions of teensy colored glints gave way to her white paws, like sand at my old swim beach.

I stopped, cocked my head and wrinkled my forehead in puzzlement. Was she real? Was this a dream? I wanted to awaken and find myself back home with my mistress and my family. I wanted to feel in control and safe in my surroundings. I closed my eyes and tried to will it so. But when I opened my eyes I was still there. The rainbow glow still pulsated and the spirit dog still faced me.

Abruptly, as though she could wait no longer, she bounded forward, and straight to me. She touched noses with me and licked my face. My mother was real! We rubbed against each other, laughed, whined, and howled our delight. I realized I was standing in the finely grained shimmers of sand with her.

"Max, my son, how I've missed you!"

"Mama! Where are we? How did you find me? Where is my mistress? Is she here too?"

"No, dear. But many you've known will join us soon. Come with me, I'll show you the way to your new home." The clouds lifted and curled around each other as they gradually revealed two structures that I had not been able to see before.

Behind my mother was a gigantic double Gate. One side stood open—she had run through it to greet me. The ornately carved Gate had been the source of light I had run towards. Multicolored precious stones inlaid in its golden swirls and turn-posts twinkled as prism-like beams radiated outward. Around the Gate the fog melted into the inviting brightness and milky clouds hovered above. The clouds and the colored glow prevented me from seeing what lay beyond, inside the Gate.

Between us and the Gate was a Bridge with two rainbows for railings on each side. It lay in front of the Gate's entrance. Under the bridge there was not water, but instead, more puffy white clouds with stars imbedded in them. Everything here was bright and sparkly.

"Follow me, Max," Mother said as she trotted over the Rainbow Bridge towards the towering shiny Gate. Her silky fur swayed, her powder white legs and delicate feet moved with easy, natural elegance. She was as beautiful to me as she had been the day my puppy eyes first opened and she was the first sight I focused on.

I was suddenly alert and excited, and did not feel sick or tired. My neck no longer hurt and the bandage had disappeared. I did not stink anymore either. I looked behind to see where I had come from. I was shocked to see a tunnel through the mists. It seemed I had cut through the fog, and a hole the width of my body tied this place to where I had been.

I saw my mistress below, where she last held me at the far end! Overjoyed that I had not lost her after all, I wagged my tailless rear end, pricked my ears, jolted upright attentively, and woofed. I wanted to tell my mistress of my recovery and the wonderful reunion with my mother.

I barked, but my mistress did not hear me. I barked again and my voice sounded as strong and deep as before the cancer took it away. But still my mistress did not respond. I saw her shoulders shaking and heard her muffled cries. She was crying as hard as when we lost Mariah. She sat on a floor with her arms wrapped tightly around a dark furry object but I could not tell what it was.

My new happiness turned to melancholy—why were we separated? Why could she not hear me? I whined and whimpered in confusion and dismay. My mistress slowly fell farther below me, and the mists began to swirl around her image. The tunnel was closing.

"Look, look! Oh, what is happening? Mistress, where are you going? Mother! Help me! I'm losing my mistress. What can I do?" I ran over the Rainbow Bridge and joined my mother at the entrance of the Gate.

"Max, you must leave your mistress. She can't join you today. But someday you'll be together again, I promise." My mother told me the same thing my mistress had when we sat by the Christmas tree. How could she know my mistress? How did my mother know what my mistress told me?

Suddenly I knew. I was dead! The fear of death I had harbored all my life had come to pass and I did not realize it until now. This was death. Yet I felt alive. I felt better than I had since I was diagnosed with cancer. The tunnel slowly disappeared as I stared, dumbfounded, and suddenly very lonely.

Then I heard other vocalizations. Yips and whines rose in volume as more dogs tumbled out of the towering Gate. Two of my brothers and one of my sisters ran towards me. I turned around again and was engulfed in an excited collision of my siblings. We whined and circled each other, rubbing our shoulders and howling with excitement. Mother smiled and watched us.

Moments later, through our rowdy rough housing I heard a familiar "Yeoowl!" I extricated myself from the tumble of dogs and saw Mariah. I stepped away from my first family and faced her, my ears forward, head up, whole body at attention, while my rear end quivered in welcome. My heart pounded with excitement, even as the horrible grief at losing her before nibbled at my joy. Was she real too?

Mariah's tail swished from side to side and she trotted on tiptoes to me, her beautiful tortoise-shell colored coat glowed and all her fur's patterns seemed lit from within her body. She wound herself through my legs as she purred and chirped.

"At last! I've missed you, dear friend." She curled around me, taking her place beneath my chest, with her head between my front legs, and her tail tickling my tummy in that old familiar way. She was here and she was real! We had not lost each other after all.

"Caw, caw, caw!" I looked to the top of the gate and there, perched on the largest curly-cue of gold, flapped Snatch. "YaHoo! Together again!" he crowed.

"Snatch!" Here was another wonderful surprise and another memory of loss made less powerful as it faded. "I'm so sorry I couldn't say goodbye. . ."

"Hey, Kid—no matter. Some other birds saw what happened and told me. But that was then and this is now." He fluffed his body, snapped out his shimmering black wings and swooped down to my back. "Come on, Kid. Let's go in."

"Let's go, Max," my brothers and sister called in unison. "Let's go *home.* Don't be afraid. We'll show you the way."

Mariah hopped out from under me and joined my mother and siblings. They trotted to the open Gate and went in. Snatch flew after them.

I remained frozen where I stood. Mother glanced back and saw I had not followed. I felt torn. This was not *my* home and I felt forced to choose between my mistress and my mother. Immobilized, I could not move forward or backward without feeling I would betray one or the other.

"Come, son." Mother tilted her head and again raised her front paw to beckon me. I swayed back and forth on my front feet, overwhelmed with indecision.

"I—I—I'm afraid, Mama!" I felt as little and helpless as I had as a puppy. Part of me wanted to run back over the Rainbow Bridge, slide into the tunnel and land in my mistress' arms—the other part of me did not want to lose my mother, siblings, bird, and cat again. I cried in desperation and flashing tears slid down my whiskers once more.

Mother's ears flicked backwards, and she cocked her head, as though she heard something. She looked backwards, towards the Gate. My tear-filled eyes followed hers.

A slouched old man in a fuzzy white robe shuffled out of the Gate and stood beside my mother. A rough rope belt knotted around his scrawny waist and he wore leather sandals on his bony feet. A scruffy, long white beard obscured his face, and scraggly gray hair half stuck out and half lay on his narrow shoulders. He held a walking stick in his right hand that sparkled like a miniature version of the Gate. When he reached my mother's side he leaned on it. His left hand stroked her marbled merle-colored head. She looked up at him with adoration in her blue eyes and they seemed to communicate without words. Then she looked at me again, smiled, and her face beamed with pride.

The old man switched the walking stick to his left hand, leaned on it, and shuffled his feet into a steady stance. Then he stood upright, raised his right arm straight out from his side and swung it in an arc until the palm of his hand rested on his chest. It was a hand signal I had learned.

In a deep, melodic voice the man said, “Max, come to me.” I could not disobey.

Epilogue

My Forever Home

I looked backward one more time. The fog deepened and obscured the tunnel. I no longer saw my mistress or heard her cry. A hole opened in my heart—a tunnel of connection through which my love for my mistress flowed to her wherever she might be. Our love for each other would bind us for eternity, yet I knew I would not see my mistress again for a long time.

I dropped my body into a submissive posture, tilted my head to the side to show respect, and arched my back as if to tuck the tail I did not have. I trotted in small steps toward the man who called me.

When I reached his feet, I folded myself into an attentive sit directly in front of him, kept my head low and did not make direct eye contact. Instinctively I knew he deserved my attention and I wanted to be polite. His large, warm hand settled between my ears. He smelled of flowers and fresh air, as though he was made of the cool night breezes of spring.

I shyly looked up into his kind pale eyes. He had an aura of sea green light about him, which caused anyone who gazed upon his face to feel washed with peace. Weathered wrinkles crinkled around his eyes and framed the strangely mischievous smile under his beard and mustache. He leaned on his jeweled walking stick with one hand again, bent over me, and with the other hand scratched behind my left ear as if he knew it was one of my favorite spots. Then the man cupped my chin in his soft hand and raised my face to his.

"I have been chosen to welcome you. Some call this place Heaven." He smiled warmly at me.

So this was Heaven! My mistress' description came back to me.

Everyone who greeted me crept back out of the Gate and sat behind the man. Snatch landed, uncharacteristically quiet, on the top. I saw no fog here; it looked bright and felt warm, although there was no sun. My mother smiled, her blue eyes full of love, and she nodded assurance to me. She walked to me again and kissed my cheek. My mother welcomed me into my new life beyond the Gate, just as she had welcomed me at my birth in my former life.

Then the man told me, "Max, you have done well. You have taken adversity and turned it into a quality life. You learned to take the gifts you were given and used them to help all species. You turned from aggressiveness and meanness and made yourself a loveable, loving animal who cared for others. You might have turned from those who hurt you and never trusted again. Instead you opened your heart to forgiveness and gave everything you could to make life better for anyone who knew you.

"You worked hard at jobs that were given to you and you were willing to sacrifice yourself to save others in danger. You remained humble in your accomplishments. You stayed steadfastly loyal and devoted to those you loved. You left the world you occupied a better, more compassionate place. You have been an excellent example of what all creatures should be, human and animal alike.

"And so it has been decided that you, of all dogs, are *special*. You deserve to be the first Watchdog of Heaven. Therefore, your job is to guide new arrivals through their fear and out of the Fog of Transition. For there is nothing more comforting than a friendly bark to help everyone find the right direction and to feel welcome to their new home. You are to sit here with me at the Gate."

Slowly the man stood up straight again, looked up into the sky at Something I could not see, smiled, and nodded. Then he reached both his bony arms up high, holding the walking stick in both hands over his head. The gems in it began to twinkle. He stood outstretched and we watched the twinkles become sparks that shot out in all directions and sprayed us in colored lights. All of us felt the warm tingles when the sparkles landed upon us. The spray increased until there were so many sparks and colors flying we could hardly see the man or each other. Immediately my indecision, fear, and confusion melted away. I knew I had finally arrived at my *one true forever home.*

Now I watch over the Gate to Heaven. I know everybody here. Everyone is kind and there is no hunger, cold weather, or rocks to throw. I visit Mother, wrestle with my siblings, watch over children, and cuddle with Mariah. I found my friend Butch and his companion Tiger. They are fun to play with and are happy to be together again. Butch's sweet mother is here for him and has become a friend of my mother's. Some of our foster dogs and several dogs from the shelter are here too. Mr. Whistler from the old folks' home introduced me to his real Shep and they are inseparable. Snatch and his flock fly by squawking, and he always swoops down to visit me at the Gate. There is no foil here, but he does not seem to miss it.

I have learned to be grateful for all the love I have known and know now. I have forgiven the meanness and cruelty I experienced in my past life. Here there is no pain, fear, anger, and no need to fight to protect myself. It is always light, never dark, scary, cold, or lonely.

I feel serene and fulfilled. I have developed the qualities of devotion, loyalty, honesty, and trust. I have learned to be a good dog—a special dog. Respected as *The Dog at the Gate*, I am proud to help all newcomers, human and animal, feel welcome.

I am especially happy to have my work. My favorite part of my job is to guide newcomers to their human or animal partners from their former lives. Nothing makes me happier than to see the joyful reunions of pets and their people who reunite in this renewed life, and help them realize they will never be separated again.

I trust that one day my last and best family will rejoin me in this beautiful, peaceful, loving place. I am patiently waiting for Miles, Muffin, Murphy, Sheba and the parakeets to join me.

But I spend most of my time next to The Gate, waiting for my beloved mistress.

Questions for Further Thought

1. Did you learn how to see the world as a pet like Max sees it? What changes can you make to treat pets with more understanding?
2. Did you know that pets become sick like people? How did you feel about Max's illness?
3. Have you lost a person or pet that you loved? Did Max's story help you feel better about the loss of your loved one? Why?
4. What were some of Max's good decisions? What happened because of those decisions?
5. Can you see the story arcs in each chapter? Why is a beginning, middle, and end of a story important? How does a main theme move the story along?
6. Max went through a lot in his life. What challenges do you face? Max turned to friends and family for support. Who do you turn to for support?
7. What do you feel were the main themes in Max's story? What messages did you hear?

For more thought-stimulating discussion points for adults & children go to www.thedogatthegate.com

Acknowledgments

Thanks beyond words go to my writing coaches and teachers at Lighthouse Writers in Denver, Colorado.

Appreciation is due to Colorado Independent Publishers Association (CIPA) who provided me with craftspeople, education, and encouragement.

More thanks go to my publishing team, without whom I would still be dreaming of becoming a published author:

- Polly Letofsky, my production manager at My Word Publishing
- Shelly Wilhelm, my editor at My Word Publishing
- Cathy Lester, my illustrator
- Kirsten Jenson, my proof-reader at My Word Publishing

- Mary Walewski, my social media coach at Buy The Book Marketing
- Corrinda Campbell, my webmistress at Hardworking Web
- Nick Zelinger, my cover designer at NZ Graphics
- Andrea Costantine, my interior designer at Self-Publishing Experts

I was moved time and again throughout my life by past writers who proclaimed themselves animal advocates before their time, including:

- Margaret Marshal Saunders, author of *Beautiful Joe*
- Marguerite Henry, author of numerous books including *Misty of Chincoteague*
- Albert Payson Terhune, author of the *Lad, a Dog* series
- Anna Sewell, author of *Black Beauty*
- Beautrix Potter, author of the *Peter Rabbit* series
- E.B. White, author of *Charlotte's Web*
- Nancy Caffry, author of *Lost Pony*

Current writers I admire who have also made the world a safer reading corner for children and a better world for animals include:

- Gary Michael, author of *Journey from Little Left*
- Kate DiCamillo, author of *Because of Win Dixie*, *The Tale of Desperaux*, and others

- Ann M. Martin, author of *A Dog's Life, the Autobiography of a Stray*
- Katherine Applegate, author of *The One and Only Ivan*

Many thanks to all the children who were my test readers and provided insightful advice, and their parents who encouraged reading in the first place.

About the Author

Sunny Weber has over 25 years of experience in animal welfare advocacy. She is a humane educator, animal behaviorist, and trainer. She believes compelling storytelling reflects her passion for seeing the world through the eyes of the animals she works with and teaches about.

Sunny has developed educational programs regarding compassion, respect, and care of domestic and wild creatures. She writes extensively on animal issues in fiction, non-fiction, and blogs.

Authors of Sunny's own childhood books influenced her future work as an advocate and writer. Consequently Sunny seeks to provide rich, multi-layered stories featuring complicated characters with whom children can identify. Her characters and their unique worlds will not only bring more understanding for pets, but also motivate children to read.

Sunny lives in Colorado with dogs, cats and parakeets. Their yard is a Certified Backyard Habitat for birds, squirrels, rabbits, pollinators, and any other creature with fur or feathers who wanders in.

Other books by Sunny: *Beyond Flight or Fight: A Compassionate Guide for Working with Fearful Dogs*

Sunny's Blogs:
www.sunnyweber.com
www.thedogatthegate.com

Made in the USA
Coppell, TX
03 February 2025

45383563R00146